INFAMOUS 1

INFAMOUS 1

#DoTheRightThing

R Cyril
West

MOLON LABE BOOKS

- Molon Labe Books –

First Edition, Paperback

West, R. Cyril
Infamous 1

ISBN 978-0-9895396-4-7
1. Coming of Age—fiction. 2. Basketball—fiction.
3. Gangs—fiction. 4. Fishing—fiction.

Library of Congress Control Number: 2018909185

Printed in the United States of America.

Author website: www.rcyrilwest.com

In memory of Ryan Hanson

Those long trips from Tucson to Seattle, battling with basketball cards, Allen Iverson vs White Chocolate, the frequent stops at Walmart to 'power-up' with new cards, inspired a novel.

"What atonement is there
for blood spilt upon
the earth?"

- Aeschylus

Day of Reckoning

"In-fa-mous... In-fa-mous... In-fa-mous..."

It's the strangest thing. In victory, with hyped-up fans chanting my fake name, instead of basking in the glory and soaking up the shine, I stare at the streak of blood on the hardwood. After a brutal game of one-on-one, it's smeared across the key like carnage from a cartel shooting.

And there's blood on my red jersey.

Blood on my shorts.

It trickles from my nose and splatters on the free-throw line.

What a game.

You won't see this on SportsCenter. A throwdown jam for the win. Crushing punishment. My latest and probably last work of artistry. But then it doesn't matter. I didn't come here to win. I came here—

"My brother," I shout. "...played his heart out on this basketball court, but lost. Two days later, he was murdered." Lifting my untucked jersey, I pull a 9mm Glock from the belly band under my shorts and flash the gun in the air. "For someone here—*for the killer*—it's game over. Because I know who you are. And I've come for justice."

Moments ago, a few thousand fans were swarming the bleachers on the other side of the chain-link fence, the steel mesh rising to form a perfect cage above my head.

Now there's nothing but stunned silence.

A killer?

Here?

All eyes on me.

Gripping the gun, my chest heaves as I stagger across the court. Breathe in, breathe out. It's the way I've been trained to overcome exhaustion. Mental toughness. That's it. Easy now. You make mistakes when you're not in control.

Bleed a little.

Bleed.

My twenty-year-old brain slips deeper and deeper into the mindset of a madman. The day of reckoning has finally come. Pointing the gun, I stop at the feet of a player with a black eye and blood oozing from his lower lip. He is lying in a daze, flat on his back amongst the shards of glass from the shattered backboard.

"Billy trusted you," I say to Miguel Ángel. "But you betrayed him."

Miguel is my ex-best friend and former teammate. He wears a flashy yellow and turquoise basketball uniform; number 30, of course. He's even tied-up metallic Curry shoes for tonight's epic clash.

Playing to the crowd.

Big mistake.

Last season, before we became enemies, Miguel and me posted a combined average 44 points and 15 assists per game.

Once, we were great.

Once, we were unstoppable.

Once, we were the best backcourt in junior college basketball.

Truth.

But this is where the mind trip begins. Because I know. I know I'm going to put a bullet in him. Ten, twenty, thirty seconds from now.

"I swear—"

"You were there," I charge, "at my house. The day he was murdered."

"Yes, but—"

"It was you. You killed him."

"No," Miguel pleads. A fresh Chupacabra tattoo lashes out from his neck. A gang symbol, I'm sure. "You got this wrong, Troy. I didn't do it."

Those frightened eyes. That cracking voice. It's a far cry from the *original gangster* thing he usually fronts.

"Who then?" I ask. "If you didn't kill him, who?"

"I can explain."

"Talk then. You got thirty seconds. Talk." I unlock the firing mechanism. "And it better be the truth."

Miguel pushes himself into a sitting position. The way he's cradling his hand, he might have broken a wrist. "Your brother came to this basketball court," he insists. "He joined the tournament. He had his sights on being the champ."

"He only wanted to beat you."

"Yes."

"For what you did to me last season."

"Yes."

"For how you destroyed my life."

"Yes." Miguel hesitates. The corners of his mouth tremor. Staring down the barrel of a gun, faced with certain death, even the strongest gangsters become mere mortals. "I'm sure that was his reason."

I wipe the sweat from my forehead. *His reason.* The words hit hard. I can't help but feel partly responsible for what happened. What kind of big brother would allow something like this to go down?

Me, of course.

Standing in silence, the tension in my stomach moves to my finger and I nudge the gun closer to his head.

From the crowd, a girl, a familiar voice of reason shouts, "Don't do it, Troy." Except I ignore her this time. Like everyone in the warehouse, she looks on in disbelief. From the bleachers, to the fans pressed up against the fence, no doubt most of these people have thought about fleeing the scene before the Mexican federales show up with their bully clubs and handcuffs; yet, they're hanging around to see what happens next.

It's not every day
    you get to watch
       someone blow
          a guy's brains out.

"Time's up," I say. "You talk too slow."

Miguel's expression tightens for an instant while he anticipates the crack of the gun.

I take a breath.

Looking at his swollen eye and the blood streaming down his neck, thinking about my dead brother, about how so much changed while I was in Alaska, I can't help but wonder: how did it come to this?

– FOUR WEEKS EARLIER –

Pursuit of Better

Once you survive thirty-foot waves on the open sea, you realize a boat is nearly bulletproof. It won't sink when deep swells and crushing whitecaps send it careening on its side or when it takes on a little water.

Troy Blake had learned this bit of seafaring physics firsthand two miles off the northwest tip of St. George Island during the last storm to strike the Bering Sea. That was when the ninety-five-foot *Romanov II*, an old slug named after a dead tsar, cut through rough water on its way to the captain's secret honey hole. The crew held on, united by a simple mantra: batten down the hatches, keep the doors closed, and stay away from the windows. It was business as usual for Captain Radanovich and his motley deckhands, including his punk nephew Ray, the prick who'd called Troy a pussy for throwing up so much.

Troy was already five and a half weeks into an eight-week stint aboard *Romanov II* and hating every minute of it. Crab fishing was the hardest thing he had ever done. Working in sub-zero temperatures just sucked. Always the burning lips. The frozen eyelashes. So yeah, he was thinking: this job's pretty much for the wild ones . . . or the crazy.

The boat dipped into a swell, came back up, and leveled out.

Wearing an orange rain jacket, bib pants, and rubber boots, Troy reached for a seven-foot high pot that hung from a hydraulic knuckle crane. The pot was made of thick steel bars and covered with nylon mesh. He guided it from an overhead pulley before opening a hatch to let the captured king crabs slide onto a metal table.

Right away, two deckhands sorted the good crabs from the throwbacks. They were young guys about his age: Carl, a lanky high school dropout from Tacoma, and Ray, the beefy, body-by-Budweiser moron from Juneau.

"Get the lead out," Radanovich shouted over a bullhorn. "Wasting time wastes fuel."

"Aye aye, Captain," Troy replied, his voice partly obscured by a scruffy beard.

From the ice-covered wheelhouse, Radanovich gazed out an open window to survey the deck's activity. He wore a black turtleneck sweater and jacket. With a groomed beard and captain's hat, he looked like Captain Nemo. The brooding man rarely spoke, except to give orders or berate the crew, which he often did over that damned bullhorn.

"And wasting fuel," Radanovich sneered, "is burning a hole in my wallet."

"Understood, sir," Troy replied, watching the crane hoist the empty trap above his head. So far today, he had helped pull fifty pots from the sea, the crew storing the empty containers on the deck, stacked in rows two layers high.

When *Romanov II* fell into another swell, a crewmember warned, "Brace yourself," before a wave of icy water rushed across the deck.

Troy slipped, clambered back to his feet, and clung onto the sorting table until the boat evened out. High on the stack of pots, a grizzled deckhand named Chuck had fallen to his knees and was holding onto the mesh.

"These waves are pressing our luck," Troy said to an older deckhand named Jimmy.

16

"Ain't it a hoot?" Jimmy shot back. His short afro was black, with gray hair dusting his sideburns and goatee.

"Ah, I'm feeling the sickness again, Jimmy."

"Hang in there, kid."

"Honestly," Troy admitted, "working at the cannery in Dutch Harbor is looking better and better these days."

"Naw, you're too good to go back to land duty."

Troy had taken several pills to fight the seasickness, but the medication had never kicked in. "I think I'm going to hurl."

"Okay, okay, but don't do it on the crabs."

"I'm serious."

"Me, too," Jimmy said. "Don't puke on the crabs. Or else the captain will dock your pay."

Troy had risen in the ranks from lowly bait-guy status, grinding up cod and salmon and jamming it into small bait jars, to learning the skills required for setting and pulling the traps. Focused and eager to learn, he was proud of how far he had come in a matter of weeks.

But the work was grueling. He wanted to quit numerous times. Fatigue was the worst. Sleeping in stints of one to three hours, he had adjusted to the sudden slap of sleep deprivation by worshipping black coffee like an island tiki.

Troy wasn't cut out for this lifestyle.

Not commercial fishing.

No way.

Thing was, he hated the frigid weather and the salty taste of the ocean air. He hated the way the boat rocked and how his head was in a constant state of vertigo. He hated eating salmon every day. Salmon in soup. Salmon in pasta. Salmon in sandwiches. Plus, there was always that smell of nasty fish guts beneath his dirty fingernails.

Work.

Nonstop work.

That was how life played out aboard the crab catcher.

Put your faith in the captain. Trust the boat. And never, ever question authority.

The totalitarian lifestyle, he thought. Just like playing for a hard-ass basketball coach. Yet, as a former hoopster and fierce competitor, Troy fed off the captain's harsh ways. He needed someone to push him. He needed someone to show him *the way*.

"You'll be happy to know," Jimmy was saying, "tonight's meal is salmon casserole."

"You can't be serious—"

"Hey, you like my salmon dishes, right?"

Troy felt his stomach turn. *Really? Salmon? Again?* When *Romanov II* crashed into another wave, his eyes crossed and he turned away from his pal and puked over the side of the rail.

By late afternoon, deluges of whitecaps upon whitecaps, like a frenzy of sharks ravaging everything in its path, threatened to shut down the boat. With only a few pots to pull, the captain would not allow the bad weather to impede progress or his fat checkbook. He rallied the crew. "Once we pull the last trap," he shouted over the bullhorn, "we're heading back to Dutch."

"He's a slave driver," Troy grumbled. "That's what ol' Rad-man is."

Jimmy shrugged. "The captain knows what he's doing."

"Yeah, I know, I know..." Troy was going on a couple hours' sleep and feeling hostile one minute, pessimistic the next. "You've been doing this for what, maybe twenty-five years now, Jimmy? How much longer you got?"

"No idea, why?"

"Is it worth it? I mean risking your life like this?"

"Sure is." Jimmy nodded. "Besides what else am I going to do?"

"Ride your motorcycle." Troy felt like he was stating the obvious. "You know, live a little."

"Ride…" Jimmy repeated dreamily. "Now you're talking, kid."

"Maybe you could visit some of those war memorials on your bucket list."

"Mmm, if only I had the time," Jimmy said. "That would be some life." Jimmy was a United States Marine Corps veteran and a member of a patriotic biker club. He rode often, mostly cruising the back roads of Alaska and Yukon Territory. "Problem is,"—a frown sucked the vision from his face—"my finances aren't too good right now. Damn spousal support. The old lady is bleeding me dry. Plus, I'm saving up for an Indian Dakota."

"Motorcycle?"

"Yup. Polished bronze. Thunder black."

"Cool. Must be a sweet ride."

"She's my dream."

"Good to have a dream, Jimmy."

The old salt nodded. "Anyway, fishing is in my blood. Has been ever since I was a youngster in Baton Rouge. It's what I do best."

"No doubt, Jimmy. You're the glue on this boat." Troy saw a buoy on the water and rubbed the sting of saltwater from his eyes.

"Speaking of which," Jimmy said, "maybe you should stick around after crab season. We're going after halibut next month."

"Ah, I have this fear of drowning," Troy admitted. "Gives me nightmares."

"You never told me."

"Sure I did."

"Oh, hell."

"Boat capsizing. Getting stuck in the cabin while the water slowly rises above my head."

"You have some imagination, kid."

"Besides, I don't think I have what it takes for the long haul."

"Maybe not," Jimmy agreed.

Troy bristled. "Hey, what's that supposed to mean?"

"What's what supposed to mean?"

"That I don't have what it takes."

"Well, you said it."

"Yeah, but don't be so quick to agree."

At a sudden whooshing sound, Troy spun around to meet a mammoth wave crashing over the bulwark. The onslaught of water sent him, along with Jimmy and Carl, careening across the deck. Holding his breath, Troy tumbled in the water, banged his head on the planks, and felt his face freeze over. Without a life jacket, he was good as dead on the open sea. Luckily, instead of going overboard he slammed against a rail and then gasped with elation as the water receded.

Jimmy and Carl were tangled at his feet.

"Man overboard," Jimmy shouted, now scrambling for the boat's life ring.

The cry ripped through Troy's ears. It was Chuck. The seasoned fisherman had vanished from the stack.

He took a step.

The boat heeled starboard.

Balancing himself, Troy raced across the deck to the launcher and searched for signs of the fallen deckhand. It was difficult to make anything out in the waves. *Where are you, Chuck?* He locked hands on the rail and swept his eyes across the sea, searching for orange weather gear and a head bobbing in the water. To his surprise, he spotted the man dangling from the stack of pots, the fishing knife in his belt caught in the webbing and momentarily saving his life.

"Oh, crap," Troy gasped, knowing exactly what he must do. Retrieving a rope, he brushed past Ray, and yelled, "C'mon. Don't just stand there. Chuck needs us!"

But Ray's glossy eyes were filled with terror, as if he were preparing himself—as if he wanted to slip into his own death and escape the impending doom before another wave hit.

Without slowing, Troy jabbed a foot into the mesh, grabbed a pot with both hands, and started up. Hand over hand. Once he began to climb, he didn't stop. Reaching the stack's second tier was like mounting an obstacle course wall. With raw athleticism, he pulled himself up and over, and then held on as the boat rocked.

You can do this, he thought, crawling to the edge of the stack. *With or without Ray's help.* He peered down at the dangling crewmate. Chuck was unconscious, his arms hanging past his head.

"Hold on, buddy," Troy called, the pots shifting and grinding under his weight. "I'm coming for you."

He worked quickly, tying a loop in the rope and sliding the other end through to fashion a harness. Next, with his teeth aching from the sea spray, he turned on his stomach, lowered over the edge, and started down.

Chuck was coming to. "What happened?" he asked groggily.

"Rogue wave," Troy yelled over the roar of water. He slid the loop over Chuck's shoulders and pulled it snug beneath his armpits.

"Goddamn. Everything happened so fast."

Troy leaned close to catch his words. "The wave caught us by surprise," he said. "Don't worry though. We got you now. It's all good." He glanced up, where Jimmy stood on the pots, holding the opposite end of the rope and securing it to the crane's boom.

A moment later, the old Cajun shouted, "Ready?"

Before Troy could answer, the boat dipped sharply, as though swallowed by a vast sinkhole, and dislodged the knife from the net. With hands gripping the rope and both legs wrapped around Chuck's body, it felt like falling off a cliff when the vessel's downward motion propelled them away from the boat.

Troy hit the water nose first.

Went under.

Resurfaced.

Gasping for air, he dragged across the water like shark bait.

Using every muscle in his forearms and biceps, he gripped the rope in the whirl of watery chaos. Defeat wasn't an option. So long as he remained locked onto the rope and the rope was connected to the crane, survival was possible. Still, he could only hold on for so long. The water was too cold; if fatigue didn't finish him off, hypothermia would, despite his thermal weather gear.

Dragging.

Gasping.

Troy realized Chuck was cradling him, too. Locked together, his hand slipped.

He inhaled a mouthful of salt water and spit it out.

Then, as though the fishing gods had heard his prayers, the rope suddenly tugged against a wave and the crane plucked their bodies from the sea.

Dangling in the air, another wave slammed them back against the hull.

Troy felt a bone pop in his hand.

It seemed like an hour passed before they were swung high above the stack of pots and the boom lowered them safely to the deck. By then, blood was oozing from a gash on Chuck's forehead. "I'm fine, I'm fine" the crew member was insisting, even though his face was ghost-white.

Troy shivered, submitting mutely as someone threw a blanket over his shoulders and led him inside the boat to warm up.

Troy pulled an elastic bandage across his blistered palm and between his swollen thumb and index finger. He wrapped several layers before securing the brace with locking tabs. After closing the medical cabinet, he passed through a companionway and entered the galley.

A long table surrounded by cheaply upholstered benches dominated the room. There was a refrigerator with United States Navy stickers on the door, a commercial coffee pot with electrical tape on its cord, and a stove with a pot of grub simmering on the burner. The galley wasn't the coziest place on earth; yet, somehow it felt like home.

Ray and Carl sat on a worn leather sofa. They were playing *Call of Duty* on a widescreen television. Watching Troy approach the stove, Ray muttered, "Hey, last time I saw something like him, I flushed it."

Carl laughed.

Troy shrugged it off and grabbed a bowl and a fork.

Two days after Christmas, the room was still decorated like Santa's wayward man cave; a singing Kris Kringle held a beer in a hand, a blow-up sex doll wore an elf costume, and a tiny white tree sat in a corner with tiny bottles of liquor for ornaments. The crew had worked through Christmas because the captain had a "tight schedule" but mostly because he didn't have any kids and wasn't particularly fond of the holidays.

Starving, Troy filled the bowl with salmon casserole. Extra pepper and gobs of parmesan helped. Right now, he would eat anything. Taking a napkin, he joined Jimmy at the table. The guy was looking at a motorcycle magazine with a cigarette between his fingers.

"Yo, what's up, seadog?"

"Hope you're hungry."

"Always. And hey, look at this. Salmon casserole." Troy slid onto a bench. "What a surprise."

"It's Mama's recipe."

"Cool. Must be good then."

Unlike other crab boats, where the crew shared in the responsibilities for meals, Jimmy oversaw provisions and always prepared breakfast and evening chow.

Troy removed a Phoenix Suns beanie from his head. "Y'know, they say you're the best cook in the fleet," he said, brushing the greasy hair from his eyes.

"Mmm..." Jimmy's apron was speckled with cream sauce. "Who

said that?"

"The captain."

"Smart man."

"Yup, and he pays well, too."

"So long as you're willing to sell your soul."

"I don't mind," Troy said with a full mouth and sauce on his beard. "A year ago I was making minimum wage at a car wash in Douglas, Arizona."

Jimmy set aside the magazine, a July edition of *Motorcycle World*. Yellow Post-its marked several pages. "Brave thing you did today," he said, eyeing the bandage on Troy's hand. "You saved Chuck's life."

"Yeah?" Troy smirked. "Well, Chuck still owes me twenty bucks for some beef jerky." He scooped casserole into his mouth and spoke with his mouth full. "What did you expect me to do?"

Ray glanced over his shoulder, eavesdropping on their conversation. He hadn't spoken a word about the near-fatal incident or even checked in with Chuck, who was suffering from mild hypothermia. The coward was probably too embarrassed. He'd had the first opportunity to act, but wet his pants.

"Well," Jimmy said to Troy, "you've got guts, kid. Just don't go thinking you're invincible or anything."

"Who, me?"

"That's how idiots get killed out here."

Brandishing a hunk of bread, Ray shouted, "Hey, this garlic bread is stale, Cookie."

"Ah, for Christ's sake," Jimmy replied.

"Is it asking too much to stock fresh food on this ship?"

"It's a flippin' boat," Jimmy said. "Not a ship. How many times do I need to tell you that?"

"Boat. Ship. Whatever. Bread's hard as a rock."

Jimmy hated when Ray called him "Cookie" but didn't let it show. How the hell the captain's nephew was even on the boat was mind-boggling.

"Shut up and eat, will ya?" Jimmy growled back. "Or next time make your own dinner."

Ray grunted before hurling the bread toward the table. It missed Jimmy by a wide margin and struck Troy on the cheek.

"Oops," Ray taunted.

Troy tossed an angry glare but kept eating. The punk wouldn't provoke him. He could control his emotions, right? Contain his anger, for once?

"Bunch of knuckleheads," Jimmy muttered before asking them to turn the volume down on the big screen.

Troy squeezed his good hand into a fist. He wanted to wipe the stupid grin off Ray's face but forced himself to remain seated. Taking a deep breath, he recalled a tip from an anger management book:

CREATE A PHYSICAL ESCAPE FROM THE SITUATION.

His ex-basketball coach at Arizona Southern College had given him the book prior to Troy's departure for Alaska, where he had swapped his basketball for a fishing knife, traded his uniform for survival gear, and, worst of all, exchanged Jordans for rubber boots.

Troy stabbed the noodles.

Truth was, he'd rather read *ESPN the Magazine*, or *Sports Illustrated*, or anything but a self-help book, yet he had read it from cover to cover.

"I've been thinking about what you said earlier today."

"Oh?"

"You might be onto something," Jimmy confessed. "About me taking some time off."

"Ah, it was just talk."

"Riding my bike across the country sounds good right about now."

"It's your dream," Troy reminded him.

"The truth is, if I had money to buy that Indian motorcycle, I'd reevaluate things."

"Good deal, Jimmy. Don't let life pass you by."

Ten minutes later, Troy wiped his mouth with the napkin and carried the bowl and fork to the sink, giving them a quick rinse before leaving the galley.

He headed for his stateroom. And he was thinking: what are you doing on a fishing boat, hauling up crab in the middle of the Bering Sea? A year ago, he was the star freshman point guard for the Arizona Southern Scorpions, on pace to set school records for steals and assists. Now *this*. Fishing.

Thing was, he had had zero experience fishing prior to joining the crew aboard *Romanov II*. Oh, he could bait a hook and throw out a line, but he hadn't grown up on the water or even near a river. Fishing wasn't in his blood. He was a dry land kind of guy, an up-tempo hoopster from Douglas, Arizona, where murderers, drug dealers, and pimps openly walked the streets. Yet, in some ways, his childhood had prepared him for the harsh conditions of the sea. Working on a crab boat, considered by many to be the most dangerous job on the planet, seemed only slightly more dangerous than life on the streets back home. Unlike other greenhorns, the dangers of being crushed by a loose pot or falling overboard or getting frostbite didn't faze him. Radanovich had even praised his "solid work ethic," insisting it was more important than fishing experience.

He encountered the captain in the companionway. The heavyset man was sucking on a cigar with a detached, menacing vibe hanging over him like a storm trapped over high mountains. Mere eye contact with the brute could crush, even kill, one's confidence. After a hesitant breath, Troy said, "Evening, sir."

"How's the hand?" Radanovich asked, looking at the gauze

bandage. His voice was surprisingly upbeat and pleasant.

"It's all good."

"Nice work today, young man."

"Thanks."

"I was wrong about you. Considering all the trouble you got yourself into back in Arizona, I figured you'd be the sorriest greenhorn I ever took on."

"I'm giving it my best shot, Captain."

"Yes, I've noticed." Radanovich slapped him on the shoulder. Was it his imagination, or did the captain always strike him harder than anyone on the boat?

As Troy reached for the stateroom's bronze door lever, Radanovich added, "I know you've got a lot going on in your head."

"Mmm..."

"You're a lot like me that way."

"I don't understand, sir."

"Life doesn't come easy for you, does it?"

"Not exactly, sir."

"Well, I admire how you haven't given up."

"Thanks."

"And so you know, I spoke to your probation officer."

Just the mention of his probation officer, like anything law enforcement related, sent chills jolting down Troy's spine. "Oh, yeah? What did ol' Officer Jack have to say?"

"He's hopeful." Radanovich blew smoke. "Hopeful you'll keep it together for eighteen more days, long enough to serve out your probation."

The captain was the only man on the boat who knew Troy had killed a man and that he served aboard *Romanov II*, and previously at the fish processing plant in Dutch Harbor, as part of a plea deal with the state of Arizona.

"And?"

"I told him you were keeping your eyes on the prize."

"I suppose that's a good thing?"

Radanovich winked. "Keep the faith, Troy. Everything will turn out good for you. You're a winner."

"Good night, Captain."

The dank smell of dirty laundry greeted Troy's nose when he entered the small stateroom. The armpit odor reminded him of playing on the basketball team, especially life in the locker room, lifting weights in the gym, and practice. He missed those glory-filled days. Now, more than ever, he felt out of place on the crab boat, isolated from his true passion and, in some ways, a prisoner aboard *Romanov II*.

Troy closed the door. Like the captain said, he had eighteen days left to walk the line between right and wrong before he was a free man again.

He stepped over a pile of motorcycle magazines and approached the bunks. The top was his and the lower one Jimmy's. A basketball rested by a pillow. He reached up and grabbed the ball, the leather cool against his hands, before walking over to a desk and sitting on a stool.

A photo of his father stood next to the desk lamp: Staff Sergeant Jeff Blake, United States Army National Guard. He was an impressive man, a civilian fireman by trade but a weekend warrior by choice. Sgt. Blake had also been an expert marksman and decorated soldier, having been awarded the Meritorious Service Medal, the Bronze Star Medal, and the Purple Heart.

Troy sighed.

It had been a stressful week. Aside from Ray's schoolboy harassment, he had accidentally dropped his iPhone overboard and, to cap things off, was thinking about his father again.

He could ignore Ray.

Purchase a new phone.

But his dad?

Taliban fighters had killed Sgt. Blake three and a half years ago in Afghanistan. Coping with the death had been hard enough. But then bombshell news dropped. A report in the *New York Times* exposed how Blake and five other U.S. Army personnel were killed searching for a deserter in the Khanabad District, a soldier who was thought to have been a prisoner-of-war.

Troy leaned back in the chair and folded his arms over the ball.

Sometimes, for brief, dreamy moments, he imagined his cell phone ringing and his dad speaking on the other end. "They messed up, son. I wasn't killed. I've been a prisoner all this time. I was captured by the Taliban. Now I've come home. Let's get tickets and go watch the Suns play."

Then the sad memories would flood back: the ceremony at Arlington; his father's casket draped in an American flag; his rifle, and a fireman's hatchet. The haunting images always slapped him back to reality.

He slammed the ball against a wall and caught it with his good hand.

Sometimes life really sucked.

He bounced the ball again and again. It made a hollow, metallic thud. Throwing it. Catching it. At some point, the thud sounded less like a basketball banging against a steel wall and more like a fist busting up someone's skull.

And with each punch...

THERE HE IS, back home in Arizona, just weeks before last season's junior college basketball tournament. And he's pounding on Miguel Ángel's face while two smaller guys try to break up the fight.

Nothing against his buddy Miguel, also known as "Destruction" to the young people crowded around the basketball court, but Troy is having a bad day. So yeah, it feels good. Unloading free-style like this. With each blow, he unloads on the traitor who deserted his post and grieves for the soldiers, especially his father, who died going after him.

The coward wasn't worth rescuing.

Punch.

He shouldn't have put his comrades at risk.

Smack.

His father didn't have to die.

Thump.

Diego, his best friend since junior high, and a pimple-faced teenage emcee whom the kids call "Taquito" grab Troy's arms and pull him away.

"Dude, control yourself," Diego says. "Calm down. It's only a game."

Troy frees himself. "No, it's freaking life."

"Yeah, I know, I know, life."

Troy wears a black jersey with the number one and the name "Outlaw" stitched across the back. Like Miguel's "Destruction" persona, Outlaw is a much larger-than-life version of himself, the baller known for in-your-face defense, for slashing attacks to the rim. The Outlaw is someone who can take a punch and deliver twice the blow. Catching his breath, he resists the urge to get in his buddy's grill, but it's difficult because only a few years after the tragedy in Afghanistan, memories of his father are passing before his eyes.

"Let's finish the basketball game," Diego says, "then go back to your house and play some Xbox."

"I'm not in the mood for computer games," Troy replies.

A sharp pain stabs near his liver. Miguel got in a few jabs, too. Why were they even fighting? For most of the one-on-one game, played on a half-court surrounded by a chain-link fence, they were pushing and shoving each other——just the way their super-charged version of basketball is played. Big thuggery. A hoops spectacle that rewards aggressive, in-your-face jams, where refs rarely call fouls, and hacking, charging, and fighting are key to a baller's arsenal.

Destruction, he recalls, mauled him at the rim. *A blatant cheap shot.* Flagrant fouls always set the stage for an altercation like this.

"No worries," Troy says, looking at Miguel, who is down on his back. "Anyway, we're cool, right?"

Miguel smirks. "Yeah, for sure, dickweed."

It's a typical Friday night at the abandoned YMCA building on the outskirts of Douglas, Arizona. The cops have closed the makeshift arena down multiple times, citing underage drinking, public disturbances, and zoning violations. But now Taquito's uncle, who owns a seedy strip club across town, manages the Extreme Hoops League like a sports franchise.

According to Diego, who always has the scoop, Mateo has bribed members of the police department to look the other way by getting them VIP tables at his strip club. Troy doesn't know or care about the details. It all sounds kind of sketchy. He doesn't do drugs. He rarely drinks alcohol. And, as far as he knows, he isn't doing anything illegal by taking part in the underground League. He just shows up to play and gets paid a hundred bucks for his effort—another fifty when he wins. *And he always wins.*

Troy pushes Taquito out of the way, saying, "Put on my basketball song, dude." Then with the back of a hand, he wipes the blood from his nose and is ready to ball.

"What's up with you?" Diego asks. "You're so mad at the world these days."

"None of your business."

"Never seen you like this."

Thinking of his father, Troy says, "You wouldn't understand."

"Try me."

"Maybe later, bro."

Miguel accepts Troy's hand when he offers help to stand, but adds, "Diego's right. You're out of control."

"Then don't climb my back."

"What the—?"

"It's about respect, dude."

Troy steps outside the cage and grabs a bottle of lime Gatorade from a gym bag. Meanwhile, his theme song, *Thunderstruck* by AC/DC, kicks in. They all have songs. Rap. Hip-hop. Techno. Troy is the only player motivated by heavy metal.

"Respect?" Miguel scoffs, the opening guitar riff droning on. "Whatever. The game ain't over."

Troy reads the digital board on the wall:

OUTLAW   DESTRUCTION

48   49

In the five months since the one-on-one League started up, no matter who he's played, former high school star or playground legend, Troy has crushed his opponents. The undefeated champion, he's 14-0.

"My ball," Troy says, tying up his kicks, retro red and white Jordans.

The heavyset referee says, "Afraid not, homeboy."

"What?"

"You walked."

"And you're freakin' high."

"You travel all the time."

Troy's eyebrows furrow. He picks up the basketball and pounds it in his hands. He is cut like a world-class athlete, with tattoos, each representing something significant in life—a state championship, West Coast recognition, his father's death.

Before sticking the whistle between his lips, the referee adds, "And I'm not letting you get away with it anymore."

"Seriously?"

"Yup."

"Yo, you need thick glasses, dude." Troy's words chase the black and white stripped guy's escaping shadow. "Any closer and Destruction would've been licking my jockstrap."

Miguel grins, and says to Troy, "Uh, so what's this *respect* thing you were talking about?"

Troy flicks him the ball.

It wasn't traveling.

Thing is, fouls are rarely called in the Extreme Hoops League. Want to smash your opponent against the fence? Or charge with a stiff forearm? Go for it. They are legit 1-v-1 basketball moves. But take an extra step? You'll likely hear the whistle for a walk.

Then again, Troy shouldn't complain. He helped make the rules. Nevertheless, he rants, "Whatever…"

A hundred young people sit in the run-down wood bleachers and many more gather at the fence.

"Thirty seconds on the game clock," the referee announces, blowing the whistle.

The music cuts.

People shout, cheer, and stomp their feet as Miguel dribbles in.

Troy gets his feet in position and attempts to slap away the ball. By League rules, you can't aggressively touch the offensive player unless he is moving toward the bucket in the act of shooting.

Playing it safe, Troy leans away, arms extended like wings, keeping his stiff back to the hoop and forcing Miguel to dribble behind the free-throw line.

With little space, Destruction makes his move by throwing up a fadeaway that bricks off the rim. The rebound comes back and lands in Miguel's hands and he tries to finish by taking the ball inside.

Until Troy slams him against the fence.

The ball bounces off the backboard and they tumble to the hardwood.

Like in Arena football, there isn't any out-of-bounds in the Extreme Hoops League. So the game plays on, the clock stopping only for timeouts, injuries, and fights.

Bouncing to his feet, Troy is a step quicker and scrambles for the loose ball, swooping it up with his left hand while smoothly maintaining a dribble so it's not traveling.

... and the final seconds tick away.

With a gap between them, maybe three feet or so, Troy steps back and jacks the ball up at the buzzer as Miguel crashes down on his shoulder. He knows it's good from the moment it leaves his fingers.

That singing whoosh.

Troy hits 51 points and the fans go crazy. His arms in the air, he stands like a monument, a youthful basketball god, energized by their cheers.

"Garbage," Miguel says in disbelief, flapping a hand in disgust.

"Like I said," Troy says with a gloating smile, "*respect*."

Diego pumps a fist, but he's also friends with Miguel so tempers his enthusiasm.

Troy says to Miguel, "I could've made that one with my eyes closed."

"Lucky shot," Miguel replies.

"Bite me."

Miguel takes a step and slugs Troy in the gut, making him buckle to a knee. "You ain't getting away with that garbage in college."

"Yeah?" Troy gasps, the wind knocked out. "But I'm still the undefeated champ of this league."

Miguel grunts. "For now, bro. For now."

TROY PULLED BACK the hood of his Under Armour hoodie before entering the crowded waterfront tavern. The festive place was glistening with silver and gold Christmas garlands. A six-point deer head hung from a wall near the entrance, with clear lights strung through the antlers.

It was 8:05 p.m. *The Vengeful One*, a song by the heavy metal band Disturbed, cranked from the jukebox. The pounding beat gave Troy a boost and slipped his adrenalin into fourth gear. The old school music brought back memories of hanging out with buddies at starlit parties, moonlit hours where huge bonfires illuminated the Palo Verde trees, their twisting green branches casting eerie shadows across the rocky desert.

He brushed by a few young guys standing at a table near the Terminator and Kiss pinball machines. They were friends from the Unalaska Processing Plant where he had worked prior to joining the crab boat. Last summer, they'd played a lot of three-on-three pick-up games at the employee basketball court on the loading dock.

"Hey," Troy said.

"What's up?"

"Not much."

"You back?"

"Yup."

Troy slapped hands and nodded but didn't stop to talk. He wasn't feeling chatty tonight. Lately, that was the best way to handle things. Instead, he marched on, slipping between people standing in the way—a group of girls, a man on crutches, some burly fishermen—and then nudged a beer drinker aside when the guy refused to move, even after Troy politely said, "Excuse me, bro."

At six foot four, he was taller than everyone in the tavern. Though he had packed on a few pounds, Troy was nevertheless in decent shape. Being tall and athletic helped in situations like these; it also helped with searching the room for Emma.

Was she here?

He scanned the shuffleboard and pool tables across the tavern, the walls plastered with NFL and Budweiser posters, until he spotted the cute blonde standing beside her boyfriend. She wore a Seattle Seahawks sweatshirt and held a cue stick in her hand.

Troy exhaled. Something about Emma's beautiful smile lit up the room like laughter from winter's darkness. Just being near her, as weird as that sounded, made him happy. Had he ever known a girl to have this effect on him?

Sweeping around a small table and passing a waitress carrying a tray of burgers, he glanced at the television above the jukebox. On *ESPN2,* a basketball game between Oklahoma and Texas Christian University ushered in ghosts from the past. Now his shoulders slackened. And he turned the other way. Troy loved basketball but found it harder and harder to watch games these days. Instead of pulling pots from the sea, smelling like fish twenty-four-seven, and wondering where next month's paycheck was coming from, he should be running the floor for a major NCAA program.

"Hey, Troy."

He heard her voice and turned around. "Emma," he said with a smile. "How's it going?"

"Great. Haven't seen you in a while."

"Work's been crazy."

"The boat?"

"Yup. Rad-man is pushing us hard."

"My dad says he always does."

"Tell me about it." Troy paused. "Heck, he's even working us through the holidays."

"Bummer."

"For sure."

"But hey, how are you liking it?" Emma was comparing the fishing boat experience to his prior position at the packaging plant across the island, where he had sliced and packed fish for twelve hours a day. She worked in the shipping and receiving department last summer, helping to manage the books. That was when he first set eyes on her, and he'd known—he'd just known—she was the girl for him.

"Well, except for a little seasickness, being on the boat is better than packing fish."

"I knew you'd be good at it."

"I do okay." He tossed her a confident grin. "Hey, when are you going back to school?"

A freshman at a small university in eastern Washington, Emma replied, "In a week and a half."

"So soon?"

"Yeah, winter break always goes by super fast."

"For sure," he agreed. "Well, too bad. Thought we might hang out some more."

"I'll be home for spring break," she said excitedly. "What about you? Will you still be here?" Maybe it was a hint at missing him ... *maybe?*

"Yup, probably." Truth was, he didn't know where he would be. A lot could change by then. As far as he was concerned, after crab season and when his probation ended, the only reason to stick around the barren streets of Dutch Harbor was to see her pretty face again. But she was taken, right? A boyfriend.

"Let's exchange phone numbers," she said.

"For sure."

Before Troy could find a pen and paper, Peter Portman strolled over. He was boorishly handsome, super smart, and had a master's degree from Oregon State University; he also held a cush management position at her father's processing plant. Peter was too stiff for this place, wearing a V-neck sweater, pleated slacks, and a work ID badge identifying him as *manager.*

"Weird," Peter said. "I smell crab." Guys like him called white trash "crabs." But the insult didn't faze Troy, who fit the part with his messy hair, unkempt beard, old jeans and a hoodie. It was just a stupid thing to say. Peter wouldn't last a day on the streets of Douglas.

"You're a funny guy, Peter Portman."

Peter grinned. "I'm only giving you a hard time."

"You got me on the ropes, bro."

"Hey, we're hiring at the plant again," the guy reported, "in case you want your old job back when you get off the boat."

Troy had worked for Peter prior to signing on with Radanovich's crew. Everything had been cool between them until it became obvious that Troy was flirting with Emma.

"Peter, Peter, Peter," Troy said, placing a hand on Emma's shoulder. "You know I'm not interested in your job. I'm interested in other things ..."

"Like what?" Peter asked with a raised eyebrow.

"Well, now that's for you to figure out." Troy winked at Emma and then walked away.

Peter.

What a loser.

What did she see in him?

Leaving the couple, he approached the tavern's long counter and slapped Jimmy on the back. His Cajun pal was hunched over a stool, working on a whiskey.

"Yo, what's up, seadog?"

"Where the hell you been?" Jimmy asked.

"You wouldn't believe it."

"Try me."

"Well, for starters, the captain wanted me to stay behind and help with paperwork."

"Paperwork?"

"Inventory stuff."

"Huh, really?"

Troy slid onto a stool. "Yeah, go figure."

"He's taking you under his wings. Bet he thinks you're going to sign up again."

"Why would he think that?"

"Well, are you?"

"I don't know. Haven't decided."

Troy hadn't let on, but he wanted to go back to college and play basketball again. Over the last few months, he had applied to small colleges in Washington and Idaho. He had high SAT scores and straight A's from his first semester at Arizona Southern. But given his troubled past, the fact that he had killed a man, was it enough? Trying to fill out the enrollment applications, even with the convenience of the internet, seemed like an impossible task with his grueling work schedule.

Jimmy sipped the whiskey. "The captain shows little love for us guys, but he thinks highly of you."

"Really?"

"Yup. He told me so. Hey, now, don't let that go to your head. He'll turn on you in a flash. You can land on his shit list with a blink of the eye."

"It's all good."

Jimmy's ashtray was full. Most people on the island ignored the law that prohibited smoking in public places, so the tavern was always smoky and reeked of tobacco.

"Anyway, your little lady," Jimmy went on, "is stretching my money."

Troy's eyes searched for Emma. If only he could hang out with her tonight. "M-my lady?" he stammered, annoyed to witness Peter with his arm slung over Emma's shoulder.

"She pours a damn stiff drink." Jimmy hoisted his glass to salute Chloe, the bartender with straight black hair down to her shoulders.

Oh, that girl, Troy thought. *The other girl.*

Many of the guys called Chloe the "Tomb Raider chick." And for good reason—the girl was a major gym rat. A black tank top showed off her toned, tattoo-covered arms. Among the many tats was a beautifully inked rose blossom on her shoulder with its stem winding behind her bicep. Ten years' worth of designs of various meanings, many of them representing hard lessons learned in life (plus an ex-boyfriend's name) told a story of sex, parties, and hardship.

"Hey, sexy," Chloe said, leaning over the counter and planting a kiss on Troy's lips. Like his, her father had died when she was in her teens, though instead of war, it was from a drug overdose. Having battled her own demons, she had been drug-free for almost two years, ever since she stopped dancing at the Last Supper Club in Anchorage.

She smiled, then went to the tapper and drew a beer. Troy was underage but good to go with his fake ID and Chloe, who was in her late 20s, working the bar. Hardly anyone was carded on the island, anyway.

Troy asked Jimmy, "I mean, don't Chloe always treat you right?"

"You betcha."

"You're a lucky man."

"If you say so."

"She's your girlfriend, right?"

"Not really."

Chloe was sweet and everything, but she had a trippy personality. Troy didn't like her probing questions, the "Where were you last night?" and, the "What were you doing?" and, "Who were you with?" Or being tied down with a relationship commitment. Besides, the girl was way too complicated for him. One day she was high on life, the next down in the doldrums.

Chloe placed a frothy pint in front of Troy. Without looking, he knew Jimmy was staring at her large breasts, at the Zen lettering tattoo—some kind of Confucius thing—that had Chinese symbols bulging from her flesh.

"I've been worried sick about you, baby," she said. "You didn't call."

"Just got in—"

"I know. But why didn't you call me?"

Troy took a sip, turning to search for Emma. "Couldn't. I lost my phone."

"Seriously?"

"It fell in the ocean. Sorry."

"It's okay, baby. Not nagging. I just missed you. That's all. Merry Christmas."

"Merry Christmas."

"Can I see you tonight after work?"

"I wish. But Rad-man has us on midnight curfew."

"What the hell, again?"

"We're heading out tomorrow."

"That guy's a real jerk for treating you the way he does."

"He's alright."

She frowned. "So ... gone for New Year's, too?"

"Yup, I told you. On the boat. Remember?"

"Okay, baby. I forgot." She kissed him again and then headed down the long countertop to serve customers. The tavern was popping with local islanders having a good time. But there was also a table of out-of-town executives in suits: bankers, accountants, lawyers. They stuck out like unwanted tourists. Especially, Troy thought, in the way they were hitting on Chloe and the other women bartenders.

"Lucky, lucky you," Jimmy was saying.

"Ah, stop with that." Troy gave Jimmy a friendly punch on the shoulder. "I'm gonna get drunk tonight. What about you?"

"What kind of a question is that?"

Again, Troy searched for Emma, arching his neck and spotting her at the pool table as she launched a ball into a side pocket. She was a shark, now and then winning twenty bucks from unsuspecting guys who thought they were better than she was. Even cooler, she was the leading scorer on her university's lacrosse team.

"It's too crowded here," Troy said, feeling cramped by people standing around him. "We got to find us a new watering hole. This place ain't what it used to be."

"Ah, hell, it's Dutch Harbor," Jimmy replied. "What else we got?"

Troy glanced at the basketball score. TCU had a five-point lead with three minutes to go. He turned away to drink. The pain was showing on his face: a loss of spirit, and, on some fractional level maybe—with the possibility of never tying up his kicks again—a reason to live.

When the game went to a commercial break, he downed his beer and waved for another.

The night would have been good like this, drinking a few brews, talking crap with Jimmy, and working up a plan to steal Emma away from her boyfriend, until he saw Ray and Carl sitting at the bar. There was a half-empty pitcher of Budwesier between them. He hadn't noticed the deckhands until now because his mind had a way of painting over their existence in broad strokes.

Ray perked up. "Hey, hotshot."

"Leave him alone," Carl insisted, his words slurred. "It's Christmastime."

"Well, *ho, ho, ho,* I'm sick of his cocky Arizona attitude." Ray killed his pint. "The douche bag has some explaining to do." He slid off the stool and walked over and stood behind Troy, breathing down his neck like a drill instructor. "Hey, I'm talking to you, hotshot."

Troy's face turned red, a flash from the past breaking through. Like a hawk soaring down on a desert rat, his mind pitched into a frenzy:

You are there, remember?

1-v-1.

The League.

Veins snake down your arms. And your bloodshot eyes are bulging from their sockets like a pop gun about to explode. Standing beneath the basketball hoop with the score 38 to 16, it's just another one of those sleepwalk kills.

You're shaking your head, annoyed by a brash point guard from Mesa State College whose downcast eyes are waving the proverbial white flag.

"Get up," you roar. "The game ain't over."

He's on a knee, catching his breath.

You call him "Socks" because of the yellow knee-highs, but he promotes himself as the "Iceman." He's a senior. Squeaky-clean. Johnny frat-boy haircut. And what the hell? There aren't any tattoos on his white skin. Must be a rich kid. Probably went to some private school in Scottsdale. You'd bet your momma's food stamps and your father's epic Metallica record collection that Socks' mother drove him to basketball practice in her fancy Mercedes Benz and made sure he always had the latest LeBron Zooms. But look at him now. Look at him. *Iceman?* There's blood on his face and his thumb is twisted from its socket. What would his mommy think? You've just kicked her sweet little baby boy's butt.

Iceman.

Some scoring threat.

Now, cut lip and all, you raise your voice, "Yo, Socks, don't be a quitter!"

Kids, most of them blazed out of their minds, cram around the basketball cage and gawk at the spectacle called you: a master ball handler. You: a three-point assassin. You: a two-fisted annihilator.

They're begging for more, and more, and more, except not for threes, or for your nasty crossover move, but for blood. They want you to go in for the kill. Remember?

Shoot.

Score.

Punch.

"I'm done," the fallen Iceman concedes. "You took it to me, bro." After talking a lot of smack on social media, warning how the "Iceman was coming for The Outlaw," he drove to Douglas with his posse to claim your one-on-one title. Second team All-Conference shooting guard? More like overrated. Either way, dude's a mess. How's he going to explain this to his coach when he rolls back to

Mesa?

"Shut up," you bark. "Get up and ball, will ya?"

"I ... I'm done."

"C'mon ... it's your ball."

When the guy stands, limping on a sore ankle, blood smeared on the Puma socks pulled to his knees, you call him a "wuss" and shove him again and he falls to the hardwood, his legs limp like boiled spaghetti.

The fans eat it up. This is their three-course meal.

Shoot.

Score.

Punch.

And you're hungry, too. You want him to keep playing, not lay down and quit.

By then, the crowd's venom is pouring gasoline onto your molten fire. Their chant a skipping record: "Fight, fight, fight!"

You don't hit players when they're down, but you're about to waste this guy when you hear Diego telling you to "chill" and you surrender to his familiar demand of bending, but not breaking. Somehow, he always manages to keep you from slipping into full berserk mode.

Easy now.

Easy.

And just like that, the Hispanic referee shouts, "No mas," and calls the game. A win by "knockout." All hail the unbeaten Outlaw, the master of the cage, the winner and undisputed champion of the Extreme Hoops League. It's not the first time you've won by busting someone's head on the hardwood. Yet you wanted fifty points. Thirty-eight is less than satisfying.

A deafening cheer grows, rocking the building. Applause for you. Praise for you. Love for you. They worship The Outlaw like some worship the Black Mamba, or King James, or Jordan. And you soak it up, feeling the moment with your eyes closed, your arms held high, letting the moment flow through your body.

Now the familiar guitar riff kicks in, blaring from the overhead speakers ... AC/DC's *Thunderstruck*.

No one can beat Troy Blake.

No one can stop The Outlaw.

You are invincible.

Troy blinked, slipping back to Dutch Harbor reality. Rising from the stool, he got in Ray's face, glared into the guy's bloodshot eyes, and snarled, "What do you want?"

A crowd had gathered.

"Show me up again," Ray slurred his words, "I'll rip your head off."

"Really?"

"I was gonna help Chuck."

"Uh-huh?" Troy shrugged. "So?"

"That's right. I was."

"Then why didn't you?"

Somewhere in the shadows, a shout, "Hit him, Ray."

And, "Do it!"

"Think you're a real badass, huh?" Ray said, pushing Troy against the counter.

Troy bounced back. "Lay off, dude."

"That a threat?"

Troy fought back the urge to land a fist on Ray's stupid face. *You've got to walk away from this. If you fight, you break your probation. If you break your probation, you go to jail.* "Look, I'm not wanting to get into it with you," he surrendered. "I came here to hang out with Jimmy. That's all."

But Ray didn't care. "C'mon, I'll let you throw the first punch. Lay it on me, hotshot."

Now people in the tavern were paying attention, including

Emma.

Relaxing his fists, Troy let out a deep breath and then calmly pulled a five-dollar bill from his wallet and dropped it on the counter. Somehow, like a man escaping the shadows of his past, he found the courage to step away from the bar, an 80s power ballad on the jukebox escorting his lowly walk of shame.

Passing Emma, he looked into the eyes of the girl he would never have. She must be thinking he was the biggest coward on the planet. Chicken-shit. Fraidy-cat. Biggest *fill in the bank* of all-time. And there was Peter, arm over her shoulder and wearing a triumphant smile that screamed:

I'm a manager.

You're white trash.

You will never get my girl.

As Troy stepped outside, and into the cold, he heard Ray's voice trailing after him, "See ya later, loser."

Troy trudged across the tavern's parking lot, passing trucks and SUVs, and entered the desolate streets of Unalaska, the largest city of the Aleutian Islands. Its modest buildings rose from windswept volcanic rock: a white church, a no-frills cannery bunkhouse, and a processing facility where scant signs of human life lay scattered along the cold waterway.

Zipped up, and with the Suns beanie keeping his ears warm, he proceeded toward the small marina located down the snow-covered street. Construction signs and a parked snowplow lined the road. He passed a historic marker that described the little-known Battle of Dutch Harbor, which took place in 1942, when the Imperial Japanese Navy launched raids on the Dutch Harbor Naval Operating Base and U.S. Army Fort Mears on Amaknak Island. Until a year ago, when he left Arizona to work in the Alaskan fishing industry, he had no idea the Japanese had attacked the United States aside from bombing Pearl Harbor.

He walked by the locked harbor master's office, its yellow vapor light flickering in the dead cold, and proceeded along a mound of snowdrift, down a metal plank, and onto a wooden walkway. Already, the sun was setting, the orange disc slipping below the fiery storm clouds and making a smoldering hell of the Pacific horizon. Fishermen aboard the mighty *Killer Queen*, a weathered vessel that had hunted king and tanner crab since the 1980s, were smoking cigarettes while working on their traps.

One of the grizzled men raised a friendly hand.

Even now, warding off his demons, those heavy voices swept up in the battle of good versus evil, the Texas Christian basketball game was on Troy's mind. Hoops was at the heart of everything.

So many what-ifs. What if his father hadn't died? What if his mother hadn't turned to drugs and alcohol to cope? What if? What the hell if?

He would never know.

His father had been there for him and Billy. He coached their Little League baseball team. He was the player to beat on the family's basketball court. Aside from his weekend obligation to the National Guard, and later during his deployment to Afghanistan, he never missed a youth game. He loved his sons but rode them hard. "Because you've got trouble in your blood," the man had warned the boys. "Your uncle was a bank robber. And a cousin is doing time in Florence for committing a murder." The Blakes, according to family legend, were descendants of William "Curly Bill" Brocius, an outlaw who'd rustled cattle back in the 1800s. "Your grandfather told me, and now I'm telling you—'stay on the good side of the law, or your ancestors will stalk your nightmares.'"

Had things turned out...

Had life gone according to plan...

Had...

Troy shook his head. Instead of packing fish and crabbing in icy water, he should be hooping it up in McKale Center at the University of Arizona, where he originally wanted to play college ball.

But following his father's death...

There was that DUI.

Stealing the principal's Dodge Charger.

And getting busted with an illegal firearm at an underage nightclub.

The list of petty crimes went on and on, and universities backed away from his recruitment. Troy was labeled "troubled," "destructive," and "do not touch." Division 1 schools quickly turned a cold shoulder on him. Coaches, athletic directors, and even recruiting services agreed: Troy Blake was damaged goods.

"Want some company?" Jimmy asked, stepping in beside Troy.

"Hey Jimmy."

"So what's the deal with you?"

"Nothing."

"How come I never seen you throw a punch?"

It was a fair question. Troy had taken a lot of heat from Ray and Carl in recent weeks. But he didn't want to open up to Jimmy and talk about his dark past. How after his father died, he had been busted for a series of minor crimes, or how he had bludgeoned a man to death. Troy wasn't proud of his criminal record or the anger that had defeated him. It was easier to keep the past locked inside his head, where the restrained two-headed monster breathed. He wanted to start with a clean slate and let the folks in Alaska judge him for his accomplishments in the fishing industry—not on the basketball court.

Jimmy knew Troy's father had served in the Army. He was equally ticked off that Sgt. Blake and his fellow comrades had died while searching for a soldier who had deserted his post. While the military bonded them, it was all the Cajun really knew about Troy's past.

In fact, Troy never spoke about playing basketball at Arizona Southern, or that scouts once considered him a top high school recruit. A simple Google search about his rising stardom would also turn up articles about his troubles with the law.

And there was Emma to consider. No telling how she would react. Would she judge him by past mistakes?

"I," Troy began, his breath turning to fog, "don't fight punks."

"Well, you're making a bad name for yourself on the boat."

"What's that supposed to mean?"

Shaking his head, Jimmy hissed, "The deckhands are calling you a pussy."

"I don't care what Ray and Carl think."

"It's not just them."

"Who else?"

"I ain't saying."

"Screw 'em." Troy folded his arms. "You don't know the first thing about it."

"Suppose we don't." Jimmy sighed. "But you shouldn't let twerps like Ray walk over you. You got to stand up to him. Push back. Or else he'll never leave you alone."

"His words are just noise to me."

"But don't you see? He's making you look like a fool."

Troy gazed into the cloudless sky, nearly dark now, the stars shining bright. He could clean this up by telling Jimmy the truth—that he used to beat guys up for thrills. That because he was on probation, if he got into an altercation with Ray, he would be in serious legal trouble. But he didn't want or even need the man's empathy. With freedom seventeen days away, it was too late for that.

Finally, Troy said, "I got my reasons for not fighting."

"Ah, sometimes you make little sense." Jimmy took a swig from a flask. "So what? What is it? You don't know how to throw a punch?"

"Sure I do."

"Is it against your religion to fight?"

49

"No." Troy took the flask. "Nothing like that."

Jimmy moaned, unable to let it go. "I hate to see you get walked on. That's all. You say you got your reasons. I respect that. But seriously, kid, if you need a lesson or two, I mean, I can show you how to fight."

"Thanks Jimmy. I'll remember that."

TIMEOUT IN THE GAME. A middle schooler with a white towel races to the free throw line and wipes up a slippery spot on the floor. Making his way to the team huddle, Troy winks at the boy and says "good job," before standing next to Jackson, his taller 6'7" African-American teammate. The Junior College basketball game is in overtime and his heart is pounding with the ferocity of a Mack truck.

This is what he lives for.

Ball *is* life.

He reads the scoreboard:

ARIZONA	YUMA CITY
SOUTHERN	COLLEGE
88	**97**

"You're playing like a bunch of fifth graders," Coach Nick Chavez rants. "Where's the defense?"

Chavez is right.

They've been getting burned on D.

With one minute and twenty seconds remaining in overtime, can the Scorpions climb back into this? *No doubt*. Troy can lead his team to victory. A quick turnover, another stop, some baskets. Anything is possible. He spots his stats on the small digital board beside the bench and exhales with frustration. Twelve points and seven assists are less than stellar.

Miguel Ángel slaps Troy's hand. "We got this, bro," he says, sporting a gruesome black eye from last night's Extreme Hoops League win against some poser from Tempe.

Troy fans himself with his jersey. He has a faint black eye, too. After the referee blows a whistle and signals for play to resume, he takes the ball from Jackson and dribbles up court. One stupid mistake—a turnover, a bad shot, too many passes—and this game is in the books. A big, fat L.

Even with a swarming defender on him, gangly arms and huge hands waving like a windmill, Troy has great floor vision. Dribbling a few feet from Coach Chavez, so close he can hear the man's racing heartbeat, he sees Miguel break for the bucket and lobs the ball up for an alley-oop jam.

Count it.

The home crowd erupts with a roar.

Troy points a finger at Miguel and pounds a fist on his chest.

On the ensuing inbound, Troy works his magic by picking off a cross-court pass, dribbles down the sideline and slashes toward the hoop for a layup.

Now down by five.

And it's crazy in the stands.

Back on defense, Troy helps double-team the Yuma shooting guard. The effort leads to a rushed shot and brick off the rim.

Troy grabs the ball in a web of hands and breaks free.

Forty seconds.

Ten guys moving the other way, almost out of gas, but laying it on the line for their schools. He holds up two fingers and calls for a play to push it inside to the team's lanky center, but gets trapped in the corner. Springing on his feet, he hurls the ball across the court to Miguel for a long three-pointer.

... which is all net.

And just like that, they're only down by two points with twenty-nine seconds to go.

Timeout Cougars.

Slapping hands.

A chest bump.

Hobbling toward his team's huddle, Troy glares at the handful of Yuma City Cougar fans in the upper rows and tugs on the front of his jersey so they can read the word SCORPIONS.

"Damnit, Troy," Chavez hollers, yanking him into the huddle before he gets called for a technical foul.

"Sorry, Coach."

At last, he's feeling the high energy. The Scorp faithful have been quiet tonight. Only now are they rising to their feet, unleashing cheers, stomping on the bleachers, and harassing the opposing team's players. Troy's ex-girlfriend Gabriela and his younger brother Billy sit behind the bench, their arms extended like a pair of conductors orchestrating frenzied chaos.

"We're out of timeouts," Chavez reminds the guys. "Now listen up, you need to step up the pressure. And don't foul. Whatever you do don't foul." He looks at Troy, and adds, "When we get the ball back, push it coast-to-coast."

"I'm on it, Coach."

As expected, the Cougars work the clock. Troy plays tight defense but doesn't risk a steal in fear of fouling. With twelve seconds on the shot clock, a Yuma player finds a lane and moves for the hoop. Troy leaves his man, and just as the player attempts to lay the ball off the glass, he blocks the shot against the backboard.

Jackson grabs the rebound and pushes the ball up the court.

Seconds now.

Crossing the mid court line, he passes the ball to Troy, who splits between two defenders and drives to the hoop for what should be an easy layup … except the ball rolls off the rim.

Missed!

What the fuck?

The buzzer sounds.

Troy drops to a knee and buries his head in his hands. He can't believe it.

How could he miss such an easy shot?

In the locker room, and sitting with a towel over his head, Troy can't escape the botched layup. A win would have given them sole possession of first place.

A shadow moves across the floor. Someone wearing shoes with colors that look like a melted ice cream sandwich is standing at his feet. He pulls the towel from his head and looks up at Miguel. His teammate must want to console him for choking—

Instead Miguel says, "Anyone ever tell you you're a ball hog?"

"A what?" Troy can't believe what he's hearing. He leads all junior college players in assists. Not to mention has the best assist to turnover ratio in the country. "Seriously?"

"Yeah, major ball hog."

He has gone from post-game blues to the edge of Hulk meltdown mode. You don't pour salt on a teammate's wounds. Troy feels bad enough that he missed an easy layup. He doesn't need this kind of B.S. from a teammate, let alone a lifelong friend.

"I was running next to you," Miguel said. "Should've passed me the ball. I don't miss layups."

Troy turns away.

It would be easy to get back in Miguel's face. Call him out for being a bad teammate. Remind him that he has had several sloppy games this season, taken numerous selfish shots, and even went on that 2-15 spurt from the charity stripe.

Except Troy is a leader.

He would never do that.

So he bites his tongue, strips down naked, and then slams the locker shut as he heads for the shower.

Within the hour he has traded his uniform for a Linkin Park concert t-shirt, Adidas high tops and faded jeans. After a quick meeting with Chavez, who tells him to keep his head up, he exits the gymnasium in a better frame of mind. Time to focus on the next game. Not dwell on tonight's loss.

Trotting down a short flight of stairs, Miguel passes Troy and makes a b-line for his girlfriend. The guy won't acknowledge Troy, or even say something like "see you later."

Troy shakes his head.

Whatever.

The need to be the game's hero is Miguel's weakness. The guy thinks he is the next Steph Curry, but he ain't even close. Miguel has bigger things to focus on, like his inflated ego and the nonstop pot smoking that has turned him into a major jerk.

Jackson and Diego tag along. Their noses are in their iPhone screens, watching the game's highlights posted on YouTube.

Troy's old Ford truck, black, muddy, and equipped with fat tires, is parked in a fire lane beneath a streetlight. Gabriela waits behind the wheel with Billy in the passenger seat.

"Crazy game," she shouts, climbing from the cab.

"No doubt," Troy replies.

"Even Michael Jordan missed an easy shot now and then."

"Sure. Thanks."

She looks at his black eye, a lingering trophy from a past cage battle, and asks, "Did Chavez ask about your eye again?"

"Yup."

"You tell him the truth?"

"Nope."

Chavez has heard rumors about the Extreme Hoops League, of its heroic champion named "The Outlaw," and has forbidden any of his players from taking part in the one-on-one games.

But lying is an act of betrayal. Hiding the truth about the underground League, especially the black eye has Troy feeling like a chump. His relationship with Coach Chavez goes back to ninth grade at Douglas High School, when Arizona, Oregon, and TCU were knocking on the door. Chavez was the rock when his father died, then somehow held the family together when Troy's basketball dreams fell apart. When he landed the job at Arizona Southern, it was under the strict condition that Troy, by then a bad seed by NCAA standards, could play for the Scorpions, regardless of his long rap sheet.

"Damn refs," Billy says. "If you ask me, I think you were fouled on that last shot." A sophomore at Douglas High, he is the starting point guard on the varsity team.

After a fist bump, Troy replies, "What's done is done."

Billy nods, then says, "Hey, where is Miguel?"

"He's not hanging out with us tonight."

"Why not?"

Billy's ongoing fascination with Miguel irks him. They all grew up together, spending summers at the neighborhood pool, playing video games, and chilling at family barbeques. Troy's father had been friends with Miguel's dad, so the families were tight in the early years of their friendship.

But the rise of the Friday night cage games has changed things. The League has a reputation as "the court of gladiators" among local high schoolers—especially with Billy and friends. Destruction has a huge following. Troy does, too. But unlike Miguel, he doesn't play the part 24/7.

"Miguel's got plans with his girl," Diego adds. "That new hottie from across the border."

"I don't like her," Gabriela says.

"We know. You've told us at least a hundred times."

"Well, why doesn't she ever hang out with us?"

"She's Mexican," Diego explains.

"So?" She points a finger at Diego. "So are you. Born in Guadalajara."

"*Mexico* Mexican. I'm a U.S. citizen. Some of them don't like American Latinos like us."

Gabriela shoves her hands into her jacket pockets. Since graduating from Douglas High, they have all maintained their relationships at Arizona Southern College. "Well, I don't like her. She's a bitch. If you ask me, she's breaking up our crew."

In the middle of a text message exchange with friends, Jackson interrupts the conversation, letting everyone know about a kegger before Diego announces his cousin has "something chill going on" at her house.

It could be one of those nights where they spend a lot of time debating what to do, only to end up down at the pool hall eating pizza and licking their wounds.

"C'mon, let's get out of here," Troy says. "We'll figure things out on the fly."

Taking a step, a sudden boom of hip-hop shakes the asphalt. A fully customized green 1963 Chevy Impala low rider has entered the parking lot with its high beams on, Mexican rap music thumping, the bass like an earthquake.

Diego perks up. "Hey, what the hell are those idiots doing here?"

"Uh-oh," Jackson says, the car rolling to a top. "Looks like we got some trouble."

Troy isn't worried. This is his turf. The guys sitting inside the Impala are members of Los Niños Machos, which translates to "The Macho Boys." They own the streets on the Mexican side of town, in Agua Prieta.

The gang's kingpin, and always the first hombre out of the car, is Juan Carlos. He wears a white tank top that shows his slate of religious tattoos. Dude thinks he looks like the heartthrob Enrique Iglesias except he looks more like a Mexican version of comedian Howie Mandel. On cue, his tall cousin José tags after him, pimped out in a Kobe Bryant jersey and with gold chains around his neck.

"Did you ladies win tonight?" Juan Carlos jibes, a gold tooth gleaming. "I didn't catch the final score."

José laughs.

Behind him, with a black Louisville Slugger baseball bat, is Pedro, a skilled rapper who goes by the name P-Fab. Because he smokes so much pot and is always half-baked Troy calls him "P-Brain."

Juan accepts a bottle of Pepe Sanchez tequila from José and takes a swig.

"Ah, get lost," Troy says. "We don't do drugs."

"Yeah, it's not our thing," Diego agrees.

"Then you're in luck," Juan says, cracking his knuckles, the gold rings and a diamond studded Rolex gleaming in the lights. "Because I'm not selling just now."

"What do you want then?" Troy asks.

Juan lights a joint and takes his time to inhale. He looks at Gabriela from head to toe with undisguised lust, eyeing her long brown hair and full lips before blowing smoke. "I have much respect for the game," he says. "It's true, when I was in prison, I coached a team with a roster that included someone who once played in the NBA's D-League and players from Mexican universities."

"And your point would be?"

"Since my release from prison, I have come to enjoy this little cage thing you have going at the YMCA."

"Yeah?"

"I've heard about you... the *great* Outlaw. The most famous one-on-one baller in the Sonoran Desert." Troy can't help but enjoy the ego-stroking. "They say you are the only player who can make a three-point shot while punching an opponent in the mouth."

Troy crosses his arms. "You've heard truth."

"I even watched you play on YouTube." Juan points a finger and, turning to his boys, adds, "He's good. He's really good, right?"

"Actually, I'm great," Troy says, growing suspicious of the praise. "What's it to you?"

"Money. Mucho, mucho dinero."

"Money?"

"Listen vaquero. How would you like to defend your cage title against my champion?"

Entertained by the offer, Troy asks, "And who would that champion be?"

Looking at José, Juan says, "My handsome cousin. Also known as 'The Big Crusher.'"

Troy erupts in laughter. *"Big Crusher?"*

"You got a problem with me, gringo?" José asks, the word "Lakers" popping from his chest as though it's the Superman logo. He stands maybe six foot three inches and, according to rumors, is a halfway decent basketball player.

Jackson is busting a gut.

"The Big Crusher?" Diego repeats. "I'll be the judge of that."

"Him?" Troy raises both eyebrows at José. "Really?"

"I don't think you appreciate my most excellent offer," Juan replies, trying to maintain control of the conversation. "Of course, there would be a generous payout to the winner. Say, five hundred dollars?"

"Five hundred?"

"Sí."

Troy considers the offer. He could use the money. His truck needs new tires. But he doesn't trust Juan Carlos. "I'm not interested," he finally says.

"One thousand."

"Still not."

"That's a lot of cash for a student to walk away from."

"Ah, get out of here."

Suddenly, Coach Chavez exits the gymnasium's back door. "Hey," he shouts with alarm. "What's going on?"

"You've disrespected me, gringo," Juan says, backing away while José and P-Brain scramble into the car. "And I don't like to be disrespected."

"Adiós," Troy taunts.

Pointing a stiff finger, Juan adds, "You haven't heard the last from me."

As the Impala drives off, Jackson grabs his crotch and yells, "Hey, Biggie, play on this!"

The car skips to the far side of the parking lot and stops, music thumping, the front of the vehicle rocking up and down. To Troy's disbelief, Miguel appears from the shadows and jumps into the backseat.

"What the—?"

Stepping up, Chavez snaps, "Who are those guys?"

"Uh, nobody," Troy says, covering for Miguel. "Just some guys asking about tonight's game."

IN ROMONOV'S GALLEY, Troy grabbed a chocolate donut and filled his thermos with coffee. His mind was dwelling on that loss to Yuma City, his last game as a college athlete. The final score had left a bad taste in his mouth. No player wanted to end his basketball career in defeat—let alone by missing an easy bucket.

"Hey kid," Radanovich's voice shattered his downcast spirits. "I've been looking for you."

Troy turned to face the bearded man. "Yo, what's up captain?"

"I need some help."

"Cool, what is it?"

"My Cuban cigars have arrived," Radanovich replied, pitching the keys to his Ford F-350 truck. "Go see Kinky Jones at the Totem Store."

"I'm all over it, sir."

"And don't waste time." The captain looked at his watch. "We're shipping out at noon."

"Understood, sir."

Wearing a heavy jacket, he pulled the Suns beanie over his ears and disembarked from the boat via a narrow plank. The temperature was in the low 30s. He found the 4x4 truck parked in the harbor's parking lot. After clearing the snow from the windshield, he hopped in behind the wheel and spun off.

Waste time? he thought, each breath looking like dragon smoke. *Who, me?*

He pulled onto the street. The beefed-up truck packed a wicked punch. The heat on full blast, he pushed the pedal and felt the truck grind over a patch of ice. For a guy who had been confined to a boat, pulling pots and cleaning fishing gear for the last two months, sitting high above the road and four-wheeling through the snow was exhilarating. And because the Dutch Harbor police rarely enforced the speed limit, he sped up and ran every stop sign along the way, unable to recall the last time he had seen a cop on the island. A traffic ticket would irk the captain, but what were the real odds of that?

First up, Troy stopped at his rented bunkhouse near the grocery store. The one-bedroom unit was surprisingly tidy and clean. While he had been fishing in the Bering Sea, Chloe had straightened things up, washing the dishes and folding his clothes; she had even put up a small Christmas tree by the television.

Walking into the bedroom (the bed made for once) he felt like a jerk for having left the Fireside Tavern without saying goodbye.

He grabbed an envelope that contained university financial aid forms, before noticing the answering machine's message light was blinking.

He hit play. It was Billy,

"Hey bro, just wondering what's up. Been trying to reach you. Everything's good. Just wanted you to know, The University of Nevada is all over me. Call when you can."

The news jacked him up. Would Nevada offer Billy a scholarship? It would be huge. The Wolf Pack were legit Top 20. And currently ranked #12 in the country.

He felt bad for not having called his brother in recent weeks. Truth was, he had been up to his neck in crab parts, getting drunk at night, and then chasing sleep. Their relationship had survived mostly on text messaging until he lost his iPhone. Now, until he could find time to buy a new phone, he was forwarding his calls to his landline's answering machine.

Troy grabbed a bag of Doritos and bolted out the door with the university financial aid paperwork, which he planned to mail from the post office near the marina.

The Totem Store was located on the waterfront a few streets away. He parked between a Jeep and a rusted-out truck. Grabbing the folder, he stepped in snow, entered the store, and walked to the counter.

"Hi there," he said to a brawny woman behind the register, "I need to talk to Kinky. He around?"

The woman looked up from a crossword puzzle. She seemed inconvenienced. "Depends. What's it about?"

"He has something for my boss."

"And who would that boss be?"

"Captain Radanovich."

A few minutes later, the seventy-something-year-old man emerged from a back room, looking like he had just woken up from a nap. Kinky rarely shaved or showered, so a foul tobacco stench followed him like black exhaust.

"Oh, yes, those cigars," Kinky mumbled. The man was so soft-spoken that Troy had to beg for silence just to hear him.

"Radanovich said they're in."

"Hmm ... no, I don't think so."

"He's usually right about these kinds of things."

Kinky scratched his head. "The captain must be mistaken."

"Can you check?" Troy was firm. "Please?" He knew the shopkeeper was a little absentminded. He also understood that coming back empty-handed would infuriate Radanovich.

"Just tell him," Kinky said, "the cigars will be in next week."

"C'mon, man, you sure? I don't want to let him down. It'll be New Year's before you know it. And we're out on the water. You know he likes to celebrate with a good cigar."

Kinky puffed on his pipe. "Hey, are you that kid from Arizona?"

"I am, sir."

"Well now, I've heard good things about you."

"Yeah?"

Kinky nodded, and then after checking his shirt pockets for something, he said, "Oh, hell, give me a few minutes to look in the back. I could be wrong."

Feeling relieved, Troy found an envelope large enough to mail the school documents, before walking to a magazine rack and picking up the latest *Sports Illustrated*. A player from Duke was on the cover. The guy was a former McDonald's All-American with serious ball handling skills, yet Troy had outplayed him at a hoops tournament in Phoenix a few years back.

Those were the days.

And he remembered...

The dream.

During Troy's junior year at Douglas High School, ESPN had listed him as the top point guard in the state of Arizona. Better yet, recruiting websites rated him four-stars, and nationally as the 89th best player in high school. In those days, offers from the biggest basketball programs on the West Coast landed on Coach Chavez's desk. Troy remembered the joyful day when he Skyped with his dad in the Kabul District, delivering the good news that he had narrowed his top three schools to Arizona, New Mexico and TCU. His father was proud. "You have the skills and talent to be the best point guard in the country," he'd said. Tragically, forty-five days later, Taliban insurgents killed the man in an ambush.

He heard Kinky say "I found the cigars" and, turning with his nose buried in the magazine, accidentally bumped into a customer.

"Sorry," Troy said, dropping to a knee to pick up the financial aid forms that spilled onto the floor.

"No worries," Emma replied, kneeling to help.

Emma?

What was she doing here?

Her bright smile sent him into a trance. "Uh, Emma. Hi."

She wore a white down jacket and knit hat. "Financial aid?" she said quizzically, looking at the paperwork. "Ugh, these forms look like a headache."

He snatched them up, embarrassed for some reason. "Yeah, sucks filling this stuff out."

"I didn't know you were going to college."

"I'm not. I mean, not exactly yet." He stuffed the last paper back into the folder.

"Hey, aren't you heading out on the water today?" she said with a raised eyebrow.

"The boat leaves in about forty-five minutes. I'm just getting the captain's cigars."

"Too bad. I was hoping maybe plans had changed."

"I wish. But, hey, maybe we can do something when I get back. You know, like hang out somewhere."

"That would be awesome."

"Cool." He wasn't shy with girls. But he was always nervous when it came to Emma. Maybe it was because he knew he couldn't get away with his normal guy stuff, like pretending to be disinterested. She was someone special. And he didn't want to play games with her.

Suddenly, two girls in the doorway called Emma's name, telling her to hurry up.

"I need some extra spending money," she said, "so I took a few shifts at the Bait Shop Café until I go back to school."

"Thought you were working at your father's cannery—"

"I needed a break from Peter. Things aren't working out between us. And I don't need the drama at my dad's office."

"Oh, good deal." And, he was thinking excitedly, *so you're single?*

The girls were growing impatient, warning Emma they would be late.

"I better go," she said.

"I'll stop by the Café when we get back next week."

"Bye, Troy."

"See ya."

Emma walked off with a schoolgirl grin, turning back to smile and wave before leaving the store with her giggling friends.

Yeah, he thought dreamily, she was *the one*.

THERE HE STANDS, hands in the front pocket of his black hoodie, gawking at an Extreme Hoops League poster on the Y's wall. Styled in post-apocalyptic art, including rattlesnakes and skulls, it promotes tonight's primetime game: Destruction, bringing a respectable 12-2 record, versus B-52, who is a perfect 6-0 in the League. The 1-v-1 game is billed as "Bloodbath I" because both players are known for going to blows and for brutal body slams against the fence.

Doomsday, Troy thinks, his ego boosted from knowing Miguel's two losses were against him. The game should be a good slugfest with plenty of in-your-face jams.

But Miguel will have his hands full tonight. Because hype aside, B-52 is a rising star. An African American hoopster from San Diego, at six-foot-five, he's a freaky dunk machine. Troy watched him play a few Fridays back and has since scoped him out on YouTube. The guy is in his late 20s. With brickyard shoulders. And pistons for arms. He played college ball but wasn't good enough to make the NBA or even ball in Europe, though he insists he played in Turkey. Then again, everyone has a story. Maybe his is true.

He spots another promo poster on the wall. This one from a few weeks ago. It shows Troy standing back-to-back with Miguel, eyes of fire, hands palming basketballs, two electrifying ballers primed for the hardwood.

OUTLAW VS DESTRUCTION
THE REMATCH

The epic rematch was the last time he had stepped into the cage for battle—when he defended his title by taking down Miguel 51-49.

His heart rate speeds up.

That fadeaway for the win.

A thing of beauty.

He pauses. Rap music plays over the building's PA system. Taquito, the Mexican American wunderkind who has scooped the crown as "best DJ in the land," spins records from a raised platform behind the hoop. Later, when the game tips off, he will play entrance songs for each competitor.

A group of young women stops next to him.

A brunette with a pixie cut says, "Hey, are you The Outlaw?"

Troy glances from his hoodie, and replies, "Yeah."

"Thought so. I recognize your face on the poster."

Admittance to the nightclub slash basketball arena is always a challenge. At the entrance, a long line of young people wraps around the building, stretching all the way to the nearby La Tapatia Market. The girls must have worked their way inside after flirting with the heavyset doorman. By their smoking hot looks, it was probably easy.

The pixie girl adds, "We heard you're a good basketball player."

"I'm all right."

"Like the champion or something."

"That what they say?"

She places a flirtatious hand on his back and whispers into his ear, "I'll be around tonight. Come find me later. Let's dance."

Under his hoodie, he wears a white Phoenix Suns jersey, Steve Nash, number thirteen. The former NBA point guard was his hoops idol as a kid. He remembers junior high when he began to mold his game after the all-star, the way he navigated the high pick-and-roll, used the dribble to attack the basket, and could get out of any jam with a left-handed behind-the-back pass.

And there was much to learn from Allen Iverson, too. Troy incorporated bits and pieces of The Answer's game, including his killer attitude and attack.

And White Chocolate ...

Lost dreams, he thinks.

Troy is not playing tonight. He blames his absence on a sprained finger, which is wrapped in medical tape. Truth is, while his finger really *is* injured and his ankle is tender, he is retiring from the Friday night cage games. Only Diego and Gabriela know about the decision, made yesterday after Coach Chavez, while grilling him about the underground basketball league and making known his suspicion that Troy was somehow involved, informed him that a Division 1 school in California was interested in his skills.

"You okay?" Diego asks, pulling him from the D1 dream.

"Yeah, I'm cool." But he's not. Being here, looking at the promotional posters on the wall, and feeling the electricity that flows from his shooting hand to his feet, he already misses the raucous crowd and the crazy excitement that rains down from the bleachers. The thrill of one-on-one "to the death" so to speak gives him a jolt he can't quite get playing for the Scorpions. But Troy knows the rules: accepting money to play violates his status as a collegiate athlete.

He groans.

How much has he made playing in the Extreme Hoops League? Less than a thousand dollars? Enough to get into trouble, he realizes. Yet he needs the cash because the shelves at home are mostly filled with rice, beans, and boxes of mac and cheese. His mom is on welfare. Because she has a thing for name-brand cigarettes and booze and expensive trips to the Bahamas, she has already gone thru most of his dad's military death gratuity.

So yeah, he thinks, *you need the money.*

Diego knocks on the men's restroom, the door marked with a handwritten CLOSED sign. A second later, a muscular Hispanic dude shows his face, throws a suspicious eye at Diego, and grumbles in Spanish, "What do you want?"

Diego's Spanish is excellent. "Dude, let us in."

"What for?"

"We want to speak to Miguel."

"He isn't talking to anyone."

"Yo, he'll talk to us."

Troy puts his hand on the door. "Open up, bro."

The bald goon looks over his shoulder then back again, before stepping aside.

Diego and Troy wander in.

Miguel is wearing a new turquoise basketball uniform with yellow shoes.

"Yo, what up, homey?" Diego says. "Fresh colors?"

"You know it," Miguel replies.

"It's most electric," Diego admits, exchanging hand slaps, "for a man of *immortal destruction*."

A Mexican with a big mustache and dressed in a suite and some black dude behind sunglasses and rocking a trench coat stand near a stall. Members of The Macho Boys. In disbelief, Troy blurts, "Dude, you said you weren't rolling with these thugs?"

67

"That what I said?"

"Yeah, exactly what you said."

Miguel grins. "Well, meet my new bodyguards."

"Bodyguards?"

"Things have changed."

"I don't understand," Diego says. "What do you mean?"

Troy doesn't like what he's hearing.

Miguel beams. "I've signed a contract with Juan Carlos."

"What the—?"

"He's my agent now."

An uncomfortable quiet prevails while the words sink in. *Agent?* Troy shakes his head. Is that really what he said? *And freakin' Juan Carlos?*

Diego smirks. "You're too much, my man. You had me going with that little joke. Agent? I almost believed you. You know hiring an agent goes against college rules."

But Troy knows he's serious.

Miguel looks at the thugs. "Show 'em," he says. The black guy, who calls himself "Mistah Krunch," slips out a roll of twenty-dollar bills from his long coat. "That's my cut of tonight's action."

"Damn," Diego says, his jaw dropping. "You for reals?"

"Oh, yeah."

Troy's heard enough. "That's just stupid," he protests. "You have an obligation. To the school. To Coach. What are you thinking?"

"I'm thinking I'm in it for me."

The news shocks Diego. He doesn't drink. Doesn't smoke. Doesn't participate in the Extreme Hoops League. He wouldn't do anything to tarnish Arizona Southern's image or hurt Coach Chavez's reputation. "Yo, Miguel Ángel," he says, sounding scared out of his wits. "You better watch what you get yourself into. This league was something fun for us to do on Friday nights. Y'know what I'm saying? Our thing."

"Well," Miguel takes the joint from Krunch, "out *thing* just went from fun to extremely profitable. Right Mistah?"

Krunch nods.

An optimist, Diego slaps hands with Miguel, and says, "Okay, good luck tonight. Destroy this guy. B-52 ain't legit. But after the game, we got to talk, bro."

Troy chokes back the anger, deciding Diego is probably right. Much better to support their teammate right now; then talk some sense into him later. He approaches Miguel and attempts to land a fist bump when his friend sticks the joint between his lips and crosses his arms.

"Not playin', eh?" Miguel asks. The words are more of an accusation.

"You know how things are." Troy holds up his bandaged finger as if the injury can speak for itself.

"That's an excuse." Miguel blows smoke and shakes his head. "You could play through the pain."

"Nope," Troy says, realizing the League has taken on new life. It reeks of organized crime. "I made Coach a promise. And I'm keeping it."

"Truth is," Miguel says, leaning into Troy's face. "Coach has been feeding your brain with lies about playing in the Big Sky. It's his way of pumping you up."

"You're wrong, dude."

"You seriously think you can ball at the next level?" He is close enough to spark a fight with a twitch of the eye. "Anyway, the answer to that question doesn't matter. Because you got a criminal record. You're tainted goods. No legit school will ever offer you a scholarship. Keep dreaming, homie."

Troy tightens up. Veins strain along his neck. He believes Chavez. He believes in the possibility of getting out of Douglas and finding a better life. Basketball is his ticket. He just needs a second chance. Someone to believe in him. "Good luck," he says matter-of-factly. "You'll need it tonight. Diego's got it wrong. B-52 is for real."

Then, thumping Diego on the chest, he walks angrily out the door.

An hour later, Troy runs into Gabriela and some of her girlfriends on the Y's second floor balcony. Back in the day, the oval balcony was a jogging track. Now it's painted light blue and has neon lights on the ceiling. From here, club-goers, most in their twenties, look down onto the hardwood court, where Destruction and B-52 are taking it to each other.

"Something is bugging you," she says to Troy. "What is it?"

"Nothing."

"I don't believe you."

"Well, guess I'm just tired of this scene," Troy finally admits. "I should be focusing on my grades and working toward playing at a bigtime university." But he is really thinking of Miguel's messed-up frame of mind. The guy is in too deep with Juan Carlos. He has accepted money for play. What's next? Any of it could jeopardize his status as a student-athlete and the basketball program itself. If Coach knew, he would go ballistic and kick Miguel off the team.

"I'm sorry," she says. "Your dreams. It must be stressful."

He tells her, "C'mon," and she follows him and Diego downstairs to the main floor. With the hood low over his eyes, Troy moves incognito past the bleachers, between rowdy fans, and into the crowd. He is feeling disappointed in himself—especially over his involvement in the one-on-one basketball league.

You messed up, he thinks. *You really messed up.* And then he moans in acceptance. Acceptance of everything.

After all, the League was his genius brainchild. Bored with Friday night desert parties, he thought it would be cool to play pick-up games at this abandoned YMCA, but with an added dimension of ballin' it rough like ancient gladiators. The fencing materials happened to be stored inside the building, so the idea of a cage surrounding the half court arena (and with no such thing as out-of-bounds) came together with little effort.

At first, the brutal games were little more than a few ballers blowing off some steam, with maybe fifteen people watching. The huge takedowns at the rim, the vicious hacks, the deliberate charges, and the fistfights were part of the fun. Just "guys being guys." At the end of the night, bloodied up and all, they were cool with each other. It was Taquito who kept track of win/loss records, suggested they create fictitious player names, organized their games as the Extreme Hoops League, and, along with his uncle, promoted the violent matches as a caged basketball league.

Fast forward to tonight. There must be five hundred people crammed inside the brick YMCA building, which sports multiple bars and a DJ booth elevated behind the basketball hoop. Mateo, and whoever else is bankrolling the League, has turned a "little fun" into a moneymaking machine.

He stands with Gabriela on one side, Diego on the other, surrounded by so-called "fans." On the hardwood, a few streaks of blood stain the floor.

You feel it.

You want it.

You can't walk away from it.

Now Troy makes his way toward the court, parting through the crowd gathered around the ten-foot-high fence. He wants a piece of the action—*he wants the winner.*

At a timeout on the floor, music by Eminem blasts over the speakers. The beat shakes the floor and rattles the recently repaired bleachers.

Now suddenly he is standing next to Jackson. His teammate's eyes are lit up. Jackson has only stepped into the cage a few times, back in the early weeks, because he plays soft and avoids confrontation. Maybe it is the alcohol fueling the guy's ego and soaking up some mindless enthusiasm, but tonight he looks to have the hunger. That *I-want-to-be-the-champ* gleam in the eye. Does

Jackson want in?

"I know what you're thinking," Troy says, exchanging high fives. "Erase those crazy thoughts, bro."

Jackson is always doing something crazy with his hair. This week, with his white girlfriend holding onto his arm, his short afro is dyed red, and he is wearing a super tight shirt with Tupac Shakur's face on it. Troy likes to say he is the Dennis Rodman of JUCO basketball, except he's not as muscular and certainly not as good a rebounder.

"I could beat Miguel."

"Don't even go there."

"You know I can." Jackson grins, sipping his mixed drink, which is probably something wussy like a fuzzy navel.

Troy grunts, dismissing the comment, and then turns his eyes back to the game as B-52 attempts to steal the ball but gets burned. Freed up, Miguel launches a three and the crowd responds with a roar. It's hard to tell who's for whom.

25-18.

"Heating up," Diego says, already forgetting about the potential trouble they are in with Coach, with the school, with the Athletic Association. "Our boy's gonna annihilate this guy."

"Heck yeah," Gabriela weighs in. "Miguel's stepped up his game tonight."

Blood Bath I is living up to its hype. And it's not just the ruthless shoving or the brief fistfight that broke out after the first play, or the flamboyant moves and killer crossovers. Rather, both players are finding their way to the rim.

And killin' it.

Troy glances over his shoulder as B-52 thumps a hand into Miguel's chest and takes it inside for a reverse jam.

"Don't let him push off," Diego shouts. "Get on him, my man."

After a turnover, B-52 has the rock again. He misses a long two-pointer, chases down the rebound, and tosses up an out-of-control shot near the free throw line as Miguel knocks him to the floor.

The basketball rolls around the rim and drops in.

"25, 22," Taquito announces over the PA system, spinning records from his turntable as the players pause to catch their breath.

A stranger recognizes Troy and asks, "Dude, how come you're not playing?"

He ignores the question. He has pinpointed B-52's weakness—an inability to shoot from the baseline—and his brain is already mapping out how easy it would be to trap him in the corner and force him to take bad shots, especially considering how out of shape the guy is. B-52's undefeated record is against players who were just average shooters in junior college, but also hustlers who sold themselves as Mixed Martial Arts competitors. Going full-throttle MMA doesn't work in the cage. Fighting is one thing, but in this League, you also have to score.

A young man with a beer in each hand slurs, "Hey everyone, look, it's The Outlaw."

More encouragements follow, like "You should be in there, champ," and "We're ready for you to crush the winner."

Any other night, he would have bathed in the glory, their praise seething in his blood like an opiate. "You're the slayer," and "You're unstoppable," and "You're the chosen one." But tonight, he is thinking:

Be smart.
Don't listen to them.
Be smart.
Walk away.
Be smart.
Go home.

Fighting his demons, blood-hot adrenaline gluing his eyes on the court, he somehow heeds his own advice and after fist bumping Jackson, breaks for the exit doors.

THICK ROPES COILED as high as a man's head gave off the smell of the ocean. It was Thursday. Troy was in his final days aboard *Romanov II*. Even better, midnight on Saturday marked the end of his probation period. Instead of focusing on pulling pots from the sea and dreaming about Emma, he was worried about his little brother. Leaving him had been the hardest part. Their mother smoked a lot of weed and she was in love with some loser from Phoenix. Troy often wondered whether his mom was paying any attention to Billy.

He turned to Jimmy. The man seemed lost in his head, too. Retrieving and stacking pots, they hadn't spoken much all afternoon. Maybe the old Cajun had a cold or something.

"Yo," Troy said. "What's up with you, seadog?"

"Nothing."

"Don't tell me 'nothing.' Something's obviously got you down."

"Oh, I get this way sometimes."

"Sometimes? But I ain't never seen you this way."

"I'm just feeling a little glum," Jimmy added, though it seemed like he was being evasive.

Troy stepped away from a pot and watched the boom carry it away. "Jimmy, you're the most upbeat person I've ever known."

"Mmm ..."

"It's true."

"Okay, since you ask," Jimmy sucked on an unlit cigar, "before we left Dutch, I got some bad news."

"Oh?"

"An old friend of mine died."

"Geez, Jimmy."

"We were Marines together."

"Sorry, I don't know what to say."

"It's life," Jimmy replied, wiping sea spray from his brow. "Bad things happen."

Troy understood. He flashed to his father. Not only do bad things happen, but they often catch you off guard. One day life is afloat, the next your ship is taking on water. He let the conversation go. Had to. He didn't want to enter those murky waters. Plus, the fishing boat was approaching another buoy, another pot, more work to do.

Then an hour passed.

King crab spilled from the traps and onto the sorting table.

At some point, Ray, who had been lollygagging most of the afternoon, stepped aside to light a cigarette, using his shoulders to shield the wind. "I need a quickie smoke," he said to the crew. "You guys handle this."

Troy huffed.

Whatever, dude.

The sea was mostly calm, a wall of gray clouds, the tail end of last night's storm, shrouding the distant Aleutian Islands. At least a hundred gulls had landed on the boat. Birds on the pots. Birds on the boom. Birds on the foghorn. When a storm blows through, birds can become caught in the winds, stuck at sea. Unable to land on the water, they fly to boats and become temporary passengers.

Troy eventually asked, "So what happened to him?"

"Him?"

"Your Marine friend."

Jimmy frowned, waving his hand for the crane operator to lift an empty pot. "The poor guy had emphysema."

"Ugh, that sucks."

"To make matters worse, the VA delayed treatment. There was a long waiting list. Or else he might have fought through it."

"Dang."

"Tell me about it, kid."

"Why do vets always get jerked around?"

From the wheelhouse, Captain Radanovich was looking out an open window. Shouting into the bullhorn, he said, "Hey, lazy nephew, put the damn cigarette out and get back to work."

Ray heaved a protesting grunt, flicked the cigarette overboard, and then returned to the table. "What a jerk off," he scoffed beneath his breath. "Old Uncle Scrooge never lets up."

Everyone except for the captain seemed burnt out.

"My lazy next of kin," Radanovich went on, "could learn a thing or two from you, Mister Blake. Keep up the good work. I'm betting on you."

Troy felt a surge of pride but hid his emotions. As it turned out, the captain was one heck of a man. Though a slave driver at times, and quick to punish lazy crew members with the least favorable tasks (like scrubbing down the holding tanks or cleaning the head) he was fair to those who were committed to the boat.

Playing basketball was one thing, Troy realized. It required commitment and drive for physical and athletic excellence.

But baiting jars?

Dropping pots?

Busting ass in frigid temperatures?

These were things he had never done, let alone imagined prior to boarding *Romanov II*. It was hard to explain to friends back in Arizona, but Troy felt like a stronger man—physically and mentally. The sea killed the weak. Only the strong survived the hardships to live and work another day. And the survivors, the men and women who bore the scars, in the mind, of the flesh, they were better off this way. He owed the captain a debt of gratitude for showing him the light.

With a blast of arctic air, Troy thumped Jimmy on the shoulder, and with tired, yet unwavering eyes, said, "Let's do this, buddy."

… then he readied himself for the next pot.

THE DOUBLEWIDE mobile home is located on three acres of cactus-filled desert, on a hill overlooking the U.S. border with Mexico. Back in the day, his father had big plans to build a family ranch on the plot of land. Shortly before his deployment to Afghanistan, and insisting it would be good for the boys to have their own court, he poured a concrete slab and installed the basketball hoop.

It's the best gift ever, Troy thinks, parking the truck next to his brother's green Geo Metro. The old Metro has a broken taillight and a cracked windshield, but at least it runs.

He jumps from the truck and heads for the front door. Trashcans along the side of the house are knocked over and garbage is strewn everywhere. The wild javelina pigs have been ravaging again.

Entering the house, Troy walks to the messy kitchen. Dishes are piled in the sink. A bottle of vodka and a shot glass sit on the counter. And an empty carton of cigarettes has fallen on the floor. He shouts, "Mom?"

"Don't waste your breath," Billy says. "She ain't home." He is sitting on the couch with a bag of Cheese Puffs and playing Madden Football on the Xbox.

"Where'd she go?"

"Out. With that douche bag."

"Larry?"

"Yup."

"What? He's in town again?"

"Ain't he always?"

Troy no longer counts on his mother for anything, except maybe to pay the bills and leave some grocery money. He works ten hours a week at a carwash. The extra cash helps.

"Great," Troy says sarcastically, grabbing a Gatorade from the fridge.

"I heard them talk about getting married and moving to Globe."

"Married?"

"Yup."

"Why would they do that?"

"I don't know."

"Ridiculous."

"For sure."

Troy plops down on the couch and grabs a video game controller. Erasing the family saga from his mind, especially images of Larry and his mom holding hands, he says, "Okay, whatever, let's play."

"Dibs on the Raiders," Billy barks out, claiming his favorite team.

"No problem. I can beat you with the Browns."

"Hardly."

"Then load it up."

"Hey," Billy says, pressing the 2-player start button. "Is it true? That you might be playing basketball in California next year?"

"Who told you that?"

"You know. The guys. Miguel."

It's supposed to be a secret. Troy isn't ready to talk about the opportunity. He doesn't want to jinx things. Might happen. Might not. Nothing is official until he receives an offer. "Well, Coach is working things out."

"Cool. You can do it. I know you can."

"Well, it's not like I've been offered a scholarship or anything."

"It'll happen."

"Hope so." He leans back into the cushion. Given his troubled past, he's keeping his fingers crossed. "Either way, it hasn't been an easy ride for me."

"Yeah, I know."

"I made some stupid mistakes," Troy cofesses. "And I regret everything."

Billy is aware of the misdemeanors Troy committed after their father's death. For the most part, his little brother is walking a straight path. Which isn't so surprising because he's a good kid.

"I know."

"Remember … Dad warned us about getting into trouble."

"I remember. 'Bad blood' in our veins." Billy shrugs like a guy who doesn't really have an opinion. Or a brother who could care less. "Ancestors 'stalking our nightmares.'"

"Yeah, well, after dad died," Troy says, "I learned the hard way."

"Mmm …"

"But thanks to Chavez things are looking up." Troy has made every effort to steer Billy in the right direction, especially in keeping him away from participating in the Extreme Hoops League.

"Dude, I know," Billy groans. "Enough with the dad lecture."

"All that fighting on Friday nights … in the cage," Troy presses on, "it's not cool."

"Yeah, yeah, so you say."

"Believe me. You have to stay focused on high school."

Now Billy perks up. "So why are you still busting guys up in the cage?"

"I'm not."

"But I heard—"

"I'm done."

"You said that before."

"I'm serious this time."

Billy rolls his eyes. "Why are you telling me this, *again?*"

"Because if the basketball scholarship is for real, I'm leaving Douglas. You'll be on your own for two years." Troy pauses for a swig of Gatorade. "And so I want you to promise me something. Promise you'll focus on school and going to college. Promise you won't get caught up playing in the cage or any other foolishness that happens in this town."

"Ah, come off it."

"Don't make the same mistakes I did."

"Whatever, dude."

"No, I'm serious." He takes Billy by the arm. "You got to keep things legit, okay?"

"C'mon, man. Everything's cool with me."

"Okay," Troy eases off, snagging the Cheese Puffs bag. *Someone must look after Billy.* "Kick the ball. Loser pays for Domino's pizza."

HEADING BACK to Dutch, Troy's mind broke free from the rigors of fishing and returned to Emma. He couldn't wait to see her. Had she really ditched her boyfriend? The plane taking her to Washington was a few days away. If he wanted to hang out with the girl, maybe go to a movie or something, he would have to act fast before she left the island.

After a dinner of indeterminate salmon casserole (not Jimmy's best dish of the week) he returned to his cabin, hoping to catch up on some z's. He found the old man sitting on the edge of his bunk, flipping through a motorcycle magazine. A half-empty bottle of Jack Daniels and a large abalone shell overflowing with cigarette butts rested near his boot.

"What's up, seadog?"

"Just looking at my dream ride," he slurred.

"Sweet."

"How was the casserole?"

"Awesome as usual," Troy lied.

"Good. Because there's plenty for leftovers to go around. Help yourself."

Troy grabbed the basketball and sat at the desk chair, seizing a quick glance of his father's Army photo. Seemed his dad was always standing over his shoulder, supplying the inspiration for working hard, for changing his ways, for fixing his dangerous mindset. "So," he said, thinking about Jimmy's dead friend, "you never talk about your past. How come?"

"Neither do you." Jimmy raised an eyebrow before handing him the bottle.

"Okay, you got me." Troy took a throat-burning swig. "I know you're from Louisiana."

"Yup."

"And divorced."

"Yup."

"Two kids."

"Bingo."

"That you're a Saints fan."

"Whodat."

Troy grinned. "I also know you like to ride." He paused to remember. "A Harley, is it?"

"Indian."

"Cool." Troy passed the bottle back. "Okay, so tell me something I don't know about you."

"Just a second ago, you didn't know I rode an Indian."

"You know what I mean. Something interesting."

"Interesting?" Jimmy set aside the magazine and thought about the question. "Well, I suppose I'm not an interesting sort of guy. Just an old fisherman. A poor black man from the bayou trying to make an honest living."

"C'mon, Jimmy. No fooling around."

Jimmy rubbed his chin and stared at the ceiling. "Well, thinking about my dead pal so much these last few days, maybe you didn't know back in the 80s, when I was in the United States Marine Corps, I was deployed to Lebanon."

"Lebanon? As in the Middle East?"

Jimmy nodded. "It was during the Lebanese civil war," he went on. "Violence was widespread. So, we Marines were there as peacekeepers." He paused, starring into the nothingness. "*Peacekeepers*. But try telling that to the damn Hezbollah terrorists."

"Oh? Why do you say that?"

"A truck bomber ..." His face was a dark canvas stained with pain. "An attack on the Marine compound. Jesus. Two hundred and twenty of my fellow Marines killed. Gone in a flash."

"Damn," Troy said. "I'm sorry, Jimmy. I don't know what to say." He was vaguely familiar with the incident. Had a teacher mentioned the terrorist attack in history class? He couldn't recall; sports and girls had occupied his mind when he should have been paying attention to academics.

"It was," Jimmy went on, "the deadliest attack against U.S. Marines since the battle of Iwo Jima during World War II."

"Terrorists suck," Troy said, reaching for the bottle.

"America lost a lot of heroes that day," Jimmy explained with glossy eyes. "Me? I lost best friends." He named them, though with an odd smile, as though remembering the good times, not the explosion, or its deadly aftermath. "Now, all these years later, I keep asking myself, why? Why didn't I die that day?"

"You can't blame yourself, Jimmy."

"My shrink at the VA tells me that, too." He frowned, smoked. "Sometimes I agree. Sometimes I don't."

"But—"

"See, thirty minutes before the bomb went off, I looked out our fourth-floor window and saw a local street vendor named Fadi. Fadi was a trustworthy young guy. A student at the American University. About your age. And Christian, I believe. Good guy. Loved Americans. Got us deals on cigarettes and local Arak."

"Arak?"

"Ah, some kind of moonshine them Arabs make."

"Oh."

"Anyway, a brother named Dejon Smith from Tulsa had collected the cash from about ten of us and was about to go downstairs and meet with Fadi when I stopped him. At the last second, I told Private Smith there had been a change of plans. 'I'm going to make the deal,' I told him. Because, you see, Fadi had a sister. Her name was Amal ... sweet, sweet Amal. I noticed she was with him that day."

"Good call, Jimmy."

The old fisherman moaned. "I only wanted to smell her sweet perfume."

"Got to respect that."

"Mmm..." He had a drink. "Five minutes after leaving the

compound with the loot, the Hezbollah truck drove into the building. Followed by that explosion. Our side of the building caved in. The concrete crushed my comrades and hundreds of others to death."

"Damn. That sucks. Geez. I'm sorry."

"I should have been one of 'em."

"You can't blame yourself."

"Somehow I can't escape it."

"But Jimmy—"

"So that's something you don't know about me. Goddamned Sunday, October 23, 1983."

Troy didn't respond. What could he say? He watched Jimmy lift the bottle to his lips. He couldn't imagine what it must be like to carry so much guilt. Yet it wasn't Jimmy's fault his comrades had died. *No way.* Even so, he understood the man's unsettled frame of mind.

They drank. Soon Jimmy spoke in hushed tones about military personnel abandoned in Vietnam. How soldiers in their seventies and eighties were still imprisoned in the jungle. He and a few buddies were planning some kind of rescue mission. He claimed Captain Radanovich, who was a ten-year U.S. Navy veteran, was in on the plan, too. At some point, the old Cajun toppled over on his pillow and tried to push himself up before passing out.

Troy moved the bottle and ashtray to the desk and then covered his friend with a blanket. "We all got our skeletons," he whispered to Jimmy, realizing his personal story of childhood delinquency, most of it brought on by selfish desires and immature ways, paled compared to his friend's real-life horror in Lebanon. "Sleep well, seadog."

Troy woke at four in the morning. Hopping off the bunk, he opened the door, thinking he might get a snack from the kitchen. When light from the hallway slipped into the room, he noticed Jimmy was no longer on his bed.

Strange.

Very strange because the captain had allotted the crew a "well-deserved break" from the grueling work schedule, giving them until seven to report on deck. It was one of the benefits of working hard and keeping ahead of schedule.

Jimmy should be sleeping, he thought. Working off a hangover. Where was he?

When Troy discovered the man wasn't in the head taking a leak, a weird sensation stole over him. Something wasn't right.

He checked everywhere—the galley, the engine room, other staterooms, and then at the helm where Radanovich sat behind the wheel smoking a cigar. "Haven't seen him," the captain said. "Did you look in the pantry?"

"Yeah, everywhere."

"What about on deck?"

"Yup. There, too."

"It ain't that big a boat. Keep searching."

"Will do," Troy said. "But hey, did you hear about his friend?"

"Mmm..." The captain nodded. "Poor bastard."

"It's got Jimmy in the dumps."

"True. And not just over his friend's death."

"Oh? What do you mean?"

"Depression." Radanovich blew smoke. "He suffers from post-traumatic stress disorder."

"PTSD?"

"Yup. Something that happened to him in Lebanon a few years back."

Having grown up in a military family, Troy knew all about the ills of trauma, in particular the strains resulting from combat. His father had volunteered to help Iraq and Afghanistan veterans who came home with PTSD symptoms. The summer before he died, Sergeant

84

Blake had organized a summer softball league in Bisbee that supported and raised awareness for his military brothers and sisters. Troy had helped coach. How much had they raised to support PTSD? Wasn't it close to $8,000?

"Hits him hard this time of year," Radanovich explained. "But he's seeing a doc. I make sure of it."

Troy nodded and returned to his stateroom, grabbed a heavy jacket from a locker, and went on deck again.

It was dark and freezing, with ice on the traps and ice covering the rails.

He looked aft, then starboard.

Still no sign of Jimmy.

The rows of pots were set high and wide and stacked with a tunnel down the middle that lead to the stern. This gave the crew a path to the back of the boat.

Had Jimmy gone in?

Grabbing a flashlight from a storage locker, he entered the long tunnel, his mind freaking over Jimmy's unknown whereabouts. Steps later, he saw the fishermen's back in the stream of light. The guy was standing on a tool box, his body well above the rail where he could easily topple over.

One little slip, he realized. And Jimmy would be gone forever. But then maybe that was his intent?

Careful of his friend's safety (don't, don't startle him) Troy crept forward until he was within arm's reach. "Stay calm, Jimmy," he repeated in his head. "Don't do something stupid." Then, reaching at the exact moment when Jimmy seemed to fall forward, Troy wrapped him up and managed to pull him to the deck.

They landed on Troy's back.

After a moment of surprise, the fallen flashlight streaming into Jimmy's face, Troy said, "Jimmy... what's going on with you?"

The Cajun just looked at him, expressionless, his skin peaked.

... the face of a lost soul.

EARLY SUNDAY MORNING. Troy has the keys to the old YMCA building and is playing two-on-two with the boys. He and Diego, skins, versus Miguel and Billy, shirts. The score is 22-17. It's supposed to be a friendly game, like last weekend when they shot around and told jokes. But today, Destruction, not Miguel Ángel, is all over him. He is throwing elbows like it's a balls-out fight to victory. With narrowed eyes, Miguel drives on Troy and delivers a vicious blow with his shoulder, before laying up the ball.

It rolls in.

Troy, his upper body and arms covered in tattoos—an angel for his father, a skull for annihilation, and a basketball on fire just because—rushes toward Miguel and throws up his hands. "What's the deal, man? I'm sick of your attitude today."

"Now what, dude?"

"You know what ..."

"Ah, give me a break." Miguel turns his back on Troy and walks away. For the last few days, he has avoided conversation about Juan Carlos and cash for play. With venom, he adds, "Bigtime ball? They're not going to treat you like a prince in Cali."

"What's that supposed to mean?"

"You figure it out."

Troy chases after Miguel when he hears footsteps near the bleachers, followed by a sarcastic Hispanic voice.

"Buenos dias, muchachos."

He turns, knowing it was directed at him. Standing at the open gate are Juan Carlos and members of Los Niños Machos, including P-Brain with a bottle of tequila and Krunch in the familiar trench coat.

Did Troy forget to lock the door? Or maybe The Macho Boys broke in.

Juan Carlos, gleaming with jewelry and that golden tooth, swaggers onto the hardwood. "Have you been to Agua Prieta lately?"

Troy shakes his head. Seriously? "What the hell do you guys want?" he says with a lion's roar.

"I've been hearing hype."

"Oh?"

"You should cross the border and listen to what all the Mexican brothers and sisters are talking about these days," Juan replies. "Outlaw the basketball god. Outlaw the champ. Outlaw the vaquero."

Billy, who is wearing an Arizona Wildcat baseball T-shirt, pipes up, "You got a problem with my brother being great? Yo, I'll be the champ someday, too."

Troy chops a hand to silence him. Billy, what did I tell you the other night? Stay away from fights like this. *Remember?* Then facing Juan, his face heated, he barks, "Go away. We're in the middle of a game."

Glowing with machismo, Juan strides over to Troy, who towers over the kingpin like the Phoenix skyline. "Do you know how it makes me feel," he asks, "to see my people put their love for you before me?" He snatches the bottle of Pepe Sanchez tequila from P-Brain. "My people need a real hero. Not a gringo. Especially a gringo who is too scared to play basketball against my champion."

Troy bounces the ball. "Ah, get lost."

"I was hoping you might have changed your mind."

"About what?"

"My offer."

"The game versus José?"

"Sí." Juan grins. "You against my cousin for the championship."

José steps from the shadows and into the cage. He is dressed in a gold Kobe Bryant Lakers jersey, purple sweats, and black Lonzo Big Baller shoes.

"It's a bad bet." Troy shakes his head. "Do yourself a favor. Keep your pesos."

He skips a bounce pass to José, who fumbles catching it. Just as he suspected, the guy is drunk. All of them, intoxicated or on drugs, including P-Brain who is wearing a Real Club España soccer shirt.

"It's unfortunate we can't agree on a game." Juan heaves a sarcastic sigh before swigging tequila. His forehead is beading with sweat, and judging by his bloodshot eyes, he seems stoned. "But why should we quarrel, eh? Why not settle this dispute today? First to twenty points."

Troy crosses his arms, and says, "Don't make me laugh."

"It's simple: if you win, I walk away." Juan throws a confident wink. "But if José wins, you come play in my town. In my cage."

"I already told you, no."

"My buddy," Diego injects, "said he ain't interested in your Big Crusher trip."

"Oh, really?"

"Yeah, really."

Shaking his head, Juan reaches behind his back and calmly brandishes a pistol.

"Dude," Troy responds, "seriously?"

"Then again maybe The Outlaw should be interested. My offer is very generous." He points the weapon at Troy. "We came here for a game, girls. We aren't leaving without one."

Moving quickly, Krunch and the gang members wrap up Diego and Billy and push them toward the gate and a set of bleachers. When Troy attempts to intervene, Juan rattles the gun, and says, "I wouldn't do that."

Now Miguel looks apologetically at Billy. "Sorry, I didn't know you'd be here."

"You knew?" Troy throws up his hands. "About this?"

Miguel starts for the exit without answering.

Troy is tempted to charge his former friend. He imagines himself doing it, but Juan might actually pull the trigger. So he goes along with the demands, watching while Diego and Billy are gagged and forced to sit with their hands bound with duct-tape behind their backs.

How is he going to protect his brother?

And Diego?

Troy glances over his shoulder. José has removed the sweatpants and is dribbling a basketball. He is a little heavy, but it looks like there was a time when he lifted weights. As if to impress, he shoots a twenty-five-footer which banks off the backboard.

Ridiculous.

Are these guys for real?

Then Troy gulps.

What the—?

Krunch has entered the cage with a long chain. A moment ago, Troy overheard him speaking with an American accent. So what's his story? He is maybe six-foot-six and looks vaguely familiar. He drops the hunk of chain on the court; a handcuff is attached to each end.

"I've been looking forward to Outlaw versus The Big Crusher for a very, very long time," Juan admits.

"What ... what's the chain for?" Troy asks.

"For you." Juan raises an eyebrow. "One cuff for your ankle."

"Huh?"

"Put it on."

"You serious?"

Juan twists his wrist and points the gun toward Diego. "Now. Or your redneck Mexican friend takes a bullet in the leg."

"You're crazy."

"Do it, cowboy!"

Troy kneels and attaches the cuff to an ankle, briefly toying with the idea of using the chain as a weapon and slinging it toward the handgun. Instead, he says with a cautious voice, "Okay, just chill, bro. I'm sure we can work something out."

"My cousin José has had too much tequila," Juan explains with a laugh, "and so this chain sort of levels the playing field."

Troy looks at Miguel. His ex-friend's eyes seem heavy with regret. Is he having second thoughts about turning on his buddies—especially Billy?

"Okay, okay, you win," Troy surrenders. "I'll come to Agua Prieta. I'll play José—"

"Too late, gringo." Juan tucks the gun into his belt while Krunch pulls the chain and fastens the other cuff to a fence post behind the hoop.

Really? They expected him to play like this? Chained up like a dog?

Troy has just enough length of chain to reach the free throw line, where, in an act of spontaneous rage, he hurls a fist at the gang leader, but misses by inches.

Juan shows a taunting grin, puts two fingers between his lips, and whistles. "Game time, muchachos!"

José doesn't hesitate. Like a horse dashing from a starting gate, he drives to the hoop and attempts to steamroll a path to the bucket. But Troy holds his position. Slowed by the clanking chain, he nevertheless gets airborne and swats away the shot.

"Oh, that's re-dick," Juan shouts with excitement, switching from captor to fan with a blink of the eye. "The famous Outlaw is even better than I imagined."

José chases down the ball and pounds it angrily on the court. Instead of attacking the rim, he dribbles to the baseline and jacks up a three-pointer, which rattles around and pops out.

Mistah Krunch shakes his head.

Troy snags the rebound, and then casually makes an uncontested basket.

"We done now?" he asks mockingly, before zipping the ball to José. "From what I can tell your game belongs on a milk carton."

"Screw you."

"Just sayin."

"Keep talking, gringo." José chases his words with a sip of

tequila. "I'm still warming up."

"Then bring your A-game, dude," Troy says, locked onto José's eyes. "Show me what The Big Crusher can do."

Dribbling near the top of the key, just out of Troy's reach, José dribbles the ball weakly between his legs once, twice, a third time. He does a weak crossover before driving to the right side of the bucket where again, and with little effort, Troy slaps away the basketball.

A string of Spanish swearwords fills the cage.

Juan covers his eyes and moans.

Enjoying the moment, Troy starts for the ball when he is blindsided by a heavy push in the back. Stumbling, he remains on his feet and throws a cocky that-all-you-got? grin at José. "What's wrong?" Troy taunts. "Mama forget to pack your game?"

"Think you're funny, huh?"

"Well, actually—"

"Do you see me laughing?"

Troy leans over, picks up the basketball with one hand, and holds it with a gleaming eye. "Your ball," he says. "Come get it." After multiple attempts to grab the basketball, which Troy swirls and sweeps out of reach, José gives up and storms away.

Speaking in Spanish, Juan rips into his cousin, telling him he is "worthless" and that even his "grandma could beat the Crusher."

Is it over?

Troy hopes so.

This whole thing is a joke. José sucks. Dude can hardly make a layup. But standing with both hands on his waist, and throwing a confident wink at his little brother, he chokes up with fear when his opponent pulls a black baseball bat from the gym bag and slashes it through the air like a deranged Jedi.

No.

Not over.

Not yet.

He underestimated Juan's intent. The Macho Boys didn't come here for a game. They came here to inflict heavy damage.

Troy retreats a few steps, keeping his distance from the slashing bat; moving until he is flat against the fence.

"You want a piece of this?" José shouts. "Huh, do ya?"

"Take it easy."

"Then forfeit the game."

Troy doesn't surrender. He can't find the words to speak. Instead, his mind is searching for an angle to take the weapon from José. "C'mon," Troy eventually pleads, "you don't want this."

He ducks when the Crusher swings for his head.

"Who's the champ now?"

"You," Troy says.

"Who?"

"C'mon, man, put down the bat."

Troy fends off another high swing before José connects against his shoulder and drops him to a knee.

"Want more?" The words fly between José's savage teeth. "Forfeit, bitch!"

Troy resists the pain spiking down his arm, and utters, "Fuck you."

A heartbeat later, José smacks the bat into Troy's face and blood squirts from his broken nose. Troy falls back and bangs his head. Blinking, dizzy, he rolls over and digs a fist into the floor before José kicks him in the ribs, and follows by stomping a foot on his shoulder blade, squashing him to the hardwood.

Blood spills from a gash above Troy's eye.

Get up, the inner voice shouts, encouraging him to his hands and knees. *And defend yourself.*

He glances over his shoulder: José has gone for another sip of tequila. Tugging on the chain, Troy can't break free. Meanwhile, the gang members are laughing and egging on his drunk opponent.

"Home run swing," Juan shouts. "Win this mother for us."

"Bottom of the ninth," Krunch adds.

Eyes lit up, José stumbles toward Troy like an executioner, the Louisville Slugger high above his head, two hands gripping the wood, and then powers down with a forceful chop.

But Troy dodges the bat. With a burst of quickness, he sweeps a leg and trips José to the hardwood.

Now both players lunge for the weapon. In the struggle for control of the bat, they tug, twist, and push each other. Within seconds, they are rising to their feet, each refusing to let go of the bat in an epic game of tug-of-war. When José flinches, Troy wrestles it away, and slams the barrel across the side of his head.

José falls to the court, blood oozing from his mouth and ear.

In a panic, P-Brain rushes up to the cage, his eyes alarmed, and shouts, "Someone coming!"

Troy staggers and feebly drops to a knee.

"Let's get out of here," Juan shouts without asking questions, the rest of the gang members already rushing toward the exit.

Miguel hesitates, unsure whom to join. His old friends? Or his new boys? Just then Mistah Krunch shrieks, "What are you waiting for, stupid?" And pushes him on.

Blood and a swollen eye blur Troy's vision.

He is pretty sure José is dead.

Hearing footsteps, he looks across the cage. It's Chavez. The coach is standing on the other side of the fence. "What the hell is going on here?" he asks, looking at the bloodied Troy, then to the dead Mexican lying on the hardwood.

Rise From Within

An alarm clock sounded at 6:45 a.m. Troy rolled out of bed. Having spent most of the last eight weeks aboard *Romanov II* battling seasickness and fatigue, it felt good to be home in his small bunkhouse lying next to Chloe's warm body.

Without opening her eyes, she mumbled something about it being "way too early," and then fell back asleep while Troy left the bedroom wearing thermals and socks.

The 1970s-era bunkhouse, one of fifty units in the cannery's two-story complex, had wood paneling and shag carpet. A big screen television, an Xbox and an Allen Iverson poster were about the only signs of modern times.

It had been a crazy night. Memories lay scattered across the coffee table: a pizza box, Chloe's cigarettes, and empty Coors Light cans. They had started the night watching movies—*Iron Man*, then part of *Any Given Sunday*—until she unzipped his pants and they found themselves naked beneath the sheets.

He flicked on the kitchen lights. The big day had finally come. Looking at a calendar pinned to a wall, he realized just how fast the year had gone by. Today was the fourth of January, the date circled in red ink and words written:

PROBATION ENDS AT MIDNIGHT

He opened the refrigerator, grabbed a carton of milk, and had a swig.

His freedom couldn't come too soon.

Next to a microwave oven, a telephone answering machine's blinking green light announced five unchecked messages.

With the back of a hand, he wiped the milk from his beard and pushed the play button:

> "It's Mom calling. Just wanted you to know I'm getting married in June. Larry will never replace your father, but he's good to me. Someday you might understand. The wedding is in Vegas. Hope you can come."

Delete.

> "This is an overdue book courtesy call from the Unalaska Library reminding you that the book *Anger Management* is past due—"

Delete.

> "Troy, where are you? We got to talk. Tonight Billy is going to—"

Delete.

> "Hey Troy, it's Gabriela. You haven't been responding to texts. Me and Diego are kind of worried. You okay? Everyone misses you. Anyway, you have my number. Also, there is something else. About Billy. It's important. Call me."

Delete.

"Troy. Jack Johnson here. I'm changing our meeting plans. Instead of Ruby's, meet me at the Bait Shop Café at 7:30 tomorrow morning. Be on time. I have an early flight to Anchorage."

Delete.

Oh, crap. The Bait Shop Café?

Wearing a black Metallica concert T-shirt and ankle socks, Chloe walked up behind him. "Who was that girl?"

"What girl?"

"Don't mess with me," she said, her eyes dark and puffy. "I heard a girl on the answering machine."

"Oh, it was just an old friend from high school."

"I don't believe you."

"What? Why not?"

"Are you cheating on me?"

Troy slipped jeans on over his thermals. "I'm telling you the truth."

"Liar."

"Jeez, what's your problem?"

"You've been distant for weeks."

Troy threw up his hands, eyebrows furrowing in frustration. "Distant? Maybe that's because I've been on a boat."

"Yeah. So?"

"And so I told you, my phone fell overboard."

Chloe seemed doubtful. And maybe for good reason. She wasn't a priority. He didn't see her as his girlfriend; she was more of a hook-up. They got together now and then. Played video games. Watched movies. Drank. Had sex. Somehow their casual relationship worked—until recently.

She went on, asking, "Where are you going right now?"

"Out," he snapped, pulling over a sweatshirt. "I have a few things

97

to do."

She stepped closer and tried to stick her hands in his pants, a trick that usually worked like a sci-fi tractor beam pulling him back to the bedroom, but he slithered away. He had to go. Jack Johnson was waiting at the café.

"C'mon, baby," she wheedled. "Let's do it some more."

He grabbed the keys from the kitchen counter and stuffed them into his pockets. "I have too much on my mind right now."

"Seriously? Since when do you have too much on your mind for sex?"

Troy heaved a moan. It was true, but instead he added, "Plus, I have to buy a new phone."

"At seven in the morning?"

Troy walked to the sofa and grabbed a heavy jacket. "No," he said. "The computer store opens at nine. First, I'm going to get something to eat."

She scowled. "You can't commit to this relationship, can you?"

"C'mon, Chloe."

"Well, you can't."

"We'll talk later."

She picked up the *Anger Management* book and hurled it toward his head. He ducked just in time, before the book crashed into a lampshade and knocked the lamp to the floor.

"You bastard. I ain't your little slut."

"Jesus, calm down."

Instead, she moved to the next available projectile, a basketball on the floor. Batting it away, he scooted quickly from the apartment.

"We're done," she yelled, as he headed down the long hallway toward the complex's interior stairwell. "Ya hear me? Done."

After she slammed the door, someone in another unit shouted out, "Shut the hell up, I'm trying to sleep."

Troy hitched a ride to the Bait Shop Café, a popular dive at the marina. Big trucks dominated the parking lot, as well as stacks of crab cages, piles of navigational buoys, and other commercial fishing gear. He thanked his driver and then walked briskly for the door.

Running ten minutes late, a blast of warm air greeted his face when he entered the crowded restaurant. He stopped at the cash register. A small sign read: WAIT TO BE SEATED.

Emma approached. Damn, this isn't good, he thought. She was working the morning shift.

"Hi, Troy," she said. Even dressed in her goofy red diner uniform Emma looked amazing.

"Hey, Emma," he responded, his eyes searching the room for a heavyset man with a greasy comb-over.

"Breakfast?"

"Yup."

"By yourself?"

"I'm meeting someone."

"A friend?"

"Uh, not exactly."

Now wasn't the time to admit he was meeting his probation officer. But when was he going to open up about the past? And how? He spotted the man sitting at a table in the far corner and told Emma he would chat with her later, then escaped. Except the escape plan had a problem: she was waiting on Jack's table. How was he going to talk about his criminal record without Emma overhearing everything?

She followed with a pot of coffee and filled Troy's cup, topping off Jack's cup, too. Good thing the guy didn't formally introduce himself, Troy thought with a relaxed breath. Emma mentioned she would be back "in a jiff" to take their order and left to help another customer.

"Cute girl," Jack said. "Know her?"

"Yeah. Her dad owns the processing plant."

"Thought I recognized her."

"She's awesome."

"So, tell me, you get in her pants yet?"

"Ah, come on, dude."

The guy wasn't exactly a role model. He liked to clown around with Troy in ways that sometimes weren't cool. Considering he was old enough to be Troy's father, some of his offhanded comments were creepy. Then again, maybe he was only trying to make a connection. Troy had gotten to know him fairly well. They met once a month in person or spoke on the phone to talk about his fishing experiences and how things were working out with his anger issues. Troy didn't open up much. Typically, would say something like, "Yeah, everything is cool," or "I'm reading a new Zen book," or offer some similar generic response. For the most part, he went through the motions, answering personal questions with as little information as possible; whatever it took to check the meeting off the list of things to do and keep the guy off his back.

Jack said, "Well, well, Mr. Blake. It's been one heck of year. Can you believe how fast time flies when you're having fun?"

"Fun? This? Uh, if you say so."

"Hey, don't look so excited."

"Just saying." A pause. "You know, fishing isn't exactly like playing basketball."

Troy grabbed the menu. They ordered breakfast—an omelet for Troy, pancakes for Jack—and talked about his days in Dutch and on *Romanov II*. Troy steered the conversation toward basketball because he knew the man was a huge Knicks fan. Better to talk about Patrick Ewing and the glory days, he thought, than Troy's personal troubles. Much easier, too.

After they ate, Jack said, "Let's make this little farewell party quick. I have official documents for you to sign. Then you're good to go."

"Sweet."

"As of midnight, if you don't get into any eleventh-hour trouble, you're a free man. Congratulations."

"Trust me. I'm good."

"And you must check in with the Arizona District Attorney's Office within thirty days."

"No problem."

"I just need to go over a few things. Then I'm going to cruise like Tom." Jack shoved documents in front of Troy, explaining what each section was about before asking him to initial here and there. "And finally," he said, "put your John Hancock on the dotted line."

"What's up with all the formalities? Feels like I'm buying a new car."

"You're buying something much more valuable, young man— you're buying back your life."

Jack excused himself and walked to the restroom.

Emma, perhaps seizing the moment to be alone with Troy, showed up to leave the receipt along with Jack's credit card. She asked, "Hey, do you still want to catch a movie?"

He lit up. "Sure do."

"Awesome. Thought maybe you might have changed your mind."

"Who, me?" Troy shook his head. "No way."

"Cool."

"How about tonight?" he asked. "You free?"

"Darn, it's my friend's birthday," she explained. "We're doing a girl's night out thing. You know, fancy crab diner with paper napkins—Dutch Harbor style. But later we're going to the Fireside Tavern to shoot some pool. Probably get there around ten o'clock. Want to meet up?"

"Heck yeah," Troy replied.

Suddenly, Jack returned to the booth, his dress shirt partially untucked. "Follow me outside," the man said, inserting the credit card into his wallet. "Let's say our formal goodbyes."

Emma's eyebrows furrowed. Did she sense something? Seeking to avoid conversation, anything concerning his criminal record, Troy raced for the door.

"So," Jack asked, zipping the jacket to his chin as they entered the frozen parking lot, "what's next for Troy Blake?"

"I want to go back to school."

"Oh, really?"

"Yes, sir."

"Good for you." They approached a Chevy Suburban, Jack's rental from the Unalaska airport. "And play basketball again?"

"You know it."

Jack grinned. "You can do it, Troy. I know you can."

"And since you asked," Troy went on, "would you mind writing a letter of recommendation? Based on your experience with me this past year?"

"Sure. I'd be honored to."

Troy retrieved a folded envelope from his back pocket. "Everything you need to know is here. The school's name, the admissions officer, and where to mail the letter."

Jack shot a fist bump. "Okay, you take care, buddy. And good luck."

As he opened the door, Troy said, "The university has a special Second Chance program. The dean of admissions knows about my arrest record."

Jack winked and climbed into the vehicle.

Troy stood there. He felt good about himself. Not only had he survived his probation—*and the treacherous days aboard the boat*—but with his life back on track, the future seemed bright. Even having taken a year off from basketball to gut fish and set traps, he didn't doubt his skills or ability to hoop it up again. Getting into a college and playing ball seemed like a real possibility.

Troy would not squander this opportunity.

He could do it.

As the Suburban pulled away, Troy noticed the shadow of a kid's sad face pressed against the inside of the vehicle's rear window. Weird. It looked like Billy.

What . . . was he seeing things?

The windows were tinted black, so it was hard to tell if it was a face or simply a reflection from the clouds.

Then as quickly as the mysterious aberration had appeared, it vanished.

Troy stuck both hands in his pockets and trudged a few blocks to the computer store. It was snowing. Making matters worse, a power outage had closed the store. Instead of getting irritated, like he would have a year ago, he chilled and took the disappointment in stride. He had gone this long without a phone, what was another day? For real, when it came down to it, he only missed being able to check the scores on ESPN.

He crossed the white street and entered a busy coffee house and ordered an Americano.

Troy remembered his dad telling him about the days before computers. "When I was a kid in the eighties," his dad would say, "we didn't have cell phones. If we wanted to play with friends, we had to walk to each other's house to see if anyone was home. That was how we rolled."

A feeling of nostalgia came over him. Funny, it used to be annoying when his dad talked about the old days like they were better days. Now he missed his father's wisdom, and those farfetched stories about walking to school in the snow—clearly lies, since his father had grown up in Tucson.

Troy smiled. He would take modern times over the 1980s any day. Throwing out a thumb, he hailed a passing truck. It occurred to him, this might be the first time since his father's death that he had ever smiled while thinking about the man.

Hopefully it would not be the last.

Unlocking the door, he stepped into the bunkhouse and set his keys and wallet on the kitchen counter. The place was trashed. It looked like a meth head had broken in and gone berserk. Leaving snow tracks, he walked to the bedroom and found the dresser drawers pulled open and his clothes strewn across the floor. Chloe's angry exclamation point, he realized, shaking his head. She had kept her promise and moved out.

Only a black panty remained in the bathroom, strung over the light fixture like dark victory, a blatant in-your-face taunt, a scream, "You'll never get in my pants again."

It hit hard.

She had been a freak in bed.

But he had to let her go.

The note in the kitchen confirmed his suspicions:

IT'S OVER. THINGS AIN'T WORKING – CHLOE

The answering machine flashed with new messages. He pushed the play button.

> "Troy. It's Gabriela. Maybe you're out fishing or something but you got to call me. It's about—"

Delete.

> "Troy. You there? C'mon, pick up. Call me—"

Delete.

What was she so worried about? Just because he hadn't called or replied to any text messages in the last few weeks didn't mean his friends had to get so freakishly upset. It was like they were keeping him on a short leash. Friends looking out for friends was cool and everything, but they were taking it too far. Whatever the problem was, he really wasn't in the mood to listen.

Life in Douglas, with all its drama and backstreet pain, seemed so distant these days. Maybe losing his cell had been a blessing in disguise. Meeting new friends, learning how to fish, and steering *Romanov II* in rough seas had him feeling rejuvenated, as though he had climbed Mt. Denali and shed new skin. Even so, after deleting the messages without listening to them, he realized he was being a dick and decided to call back.

As he dialed Gabriela's number he heard a crash and, dropping the phone, raced to the window. Two cars, a Range Rover and a Pathfinder, had rammed into each other on a patch of ice in the apartment complex's parking lot. The drivers climbed from their dented vehicles to inspect the damage; it appeared everyone was okay. He returned to the kitchen, hung up the phone, and made a sandwich.

Hours later, after watching ESPN's *30 for 30*, walking to the library to use the computer, and then falling asleep until ten, he realized that he had forgotten to call Gabriela back.

By then he was on his way to the Fireside Tavern.

Would Emma be there?

He arrived at 11:15 p.m. The tavern was packed, the Kiss pinball machine lit up, the 1950s replica jukebox thumping with old school rock.

He spotted Emma right away. She was sitting at a booth by the pool table, surrounded by friends.

And Peter was there, too.

Great, he thought, feeling let down.

Weren't they broken up?

He walked to the jukebox and inserted several quarters. Maybe

105

Emma was messing with him. Maybe she wasn't really interested. He was searching through the songs when she came over and said, "Sorry, I didn't know Peter would crash the party."

"It's cool."

"We aren't together anymore, but it's awkward. I can't ask him to leave because he's Tanya's friend, too."

"No problem." Troy understood and didn't want to put any pressure on her. "It's early. We'll talk later."

"I'd like that," she replied.

He smiled, and jested, "I'll give you forty-five minutes to wrap things up."

"You're awesome."

Someone shouted to Emma that it was her "turn to shoot."

"You better go," Troy said, placing a hand on her shoulder.

"I'll talk to you," she replied, "at the stroke of midnight."

He smiled. "See ya, Cinderella."

After she walked away, he looked across the room toward the bar where Ray and Carl sat hunched over pints, and watched Chloe set a bowl of peanuts on the counter. Then, her eyes homing in on Troy with heat-seeking accuracy, she leaned over and planted a long kiss on Ray's lips; the kiss gathered some oohs and aahs from patrons sitting nearby.

Jealous?

Troy?

No.

He dropped more quarters into the machine and selected several songs, most of them classic rock, before joining Jimmy at the bustling counter.

"What're you drinking, my man?" Troy asked.

"The usual," Jimmy replied.

Another waitress was serving Troy because Chloe was keeping her distance.

"You and the babe in some kind of fight?"

"Yeah."

"What's the problem?"

"Ah, I don't want to get into it."

"Okie-dokie."

"Besides, like I told you, she isn't my girlfriend."

Jimmy placed a hand on Troy's shoulder, a gesture that seemed heartfelt. "Say, I can't thank you enough for what you did the other day. First Chuck. Now me."

"Just doing my part."

In the aftermath, they had briefly spoken about Jimmy's suicide attempt, about his ongoing struggles with PTSD, but the old Cajun had eventually held up a hand to put an end to the conversation. He was seeking help at the VA hospital. That was how he wanted to leave things.

"Well, I've been thinking," he went on. "A few nights ago, I told you about my dream. The Indian bike. Riding coast to coast."

"Yeah, that's some sweet dream." Troy paused for his beer. "If I had the cash, I'd buy that motorcycle for you."

Jimmy nodded. "What about you? What's your dream?"

"Oh, I don't know."

"You've got grit, kid. But to be honest, it's clear fishing isn't in your blood."

"Why do you say that?"

"For starters, there's the seasickness thing."

"True."

"And you're not exactly a huge fan of my casserole."

"How'd you know?"

"I just know. But you're a good sport about what we eat on the boat. I'll give you that."

Busted, Troy cracked a smile. "Honestly, it's just—"

"So you must have dreams." Jimmy lit a cigarette. "What do you want to do with your life besides pretend to be a fisherman?"

Troy's eyes searched for Emma, then glanced up to the

television above the shelves of booze where a player from the UCLA Bruins was doing a post-game interview.

"Truth is," he said, feeling it, recognizing it, believing it. "I want to play college basketball."

"Basketball?"

"You got it, seadog."

Jimmy nearly choked on his drink. "No seriously, Troy. Your dream? What is it?"

"I am serious."

Troy waved his hand to a woman bartender and signaled for another round. A Jack and Coke for Jimmy, and a shot of tequila for him. Then he told his pal everything—about his high school ballin' days, how he was once rated a top point guard in the country, followed by the big downfall after his father died.

And he didn't stop there. Troy relived his freshman season at Arizona Southern College and watched the man's eyes grow wide as he learned about the mighty Outlaw, the brutal fistfights in the cage, and the day he killed José in self-defense.

"So all this time, you've been on probation?"

"Yup."

"Captain know?"

Troy nodded. "This is why I've been avoiding confrontation with Ray."

"And you," Jimmy stammered, "really killed someone?"

"I ain't exactly proud of it."

"Boy, do I feel stupid."

"Why?"

"Because I volunteered to teach you how to fight."

Troy raised his pint for a toast. "I'm sure you could teach me a thing or two."

"Oh, sweet Jesus."

"But hey …" He looked at his watch, *Teen Spirit*, by Nirvana kicking in at 11:45 p.m. "I'm a free man in exactly fifteen minutes.

Time to celebrate."

Troy had to take a leak so went to the men's restroom.

He unzipped his pants and stood at the urinal. It was also time, he decided, to make his move and rescue Emma from the party. Maybe she would want to walk to the Harbor View Lounge. The lounge was a quiet place, with mood lighting and a piano player on Tuesday nights; perfect for just sitting and talking.

He was making plans in his head when Ray emerged from a stall. Troy held his breath. The moment was awkward. Stuck in a stalemate, neither had spoken more than a few words to each other since their last bar room altercation.

Belching, Ray checked himself out in the mirror.

What an idiot, Troy thought.

When the d-bag left without washing his hands, he flicked off the light switch, stranding Troy in the dark.

Jerk.

Zipping up, then exiting the restroom with hands in fists, Troy glanced at his watch. It was midnight. High noon. According to the law, he was free at last.

Yet, of all things, Peter was waiting outside the door. "I don't know what you said to Emma," he blurted with an intoxicated glaze, "but she's still my girl."

"What?" Troy didn't have time for this.

"We're just working through some relationship stuff."

"Okay. Cool. Whatever."

He brushed Peter aside, but the angry guy trailed after him. "Hey, wait," Peter persisted, "I'm talking to you."

"Not now, dude."

"But—"

Troy had other things on his mind. Ray turning off the bathroom's light was the last straw. The punk had pushed him too far. At the bar, making matters worse, he found the guy sitting on the stool next to Jimmy.

"Dude, you're in my seat," Troy said.

Ray looked over his shoulder with a twisted grin. "What do you want, loser?"

"I said, that's my stool."

Peter was fuming, still rambling into Troy's ear about "laying off" his girl.

"Funny," Ray jibbed, looking sarcastically at the barstool. "I don't see your name on it."

"Don't be a tool."

People were catching wind of a brewing fight and started to gather. Someone said, "Hit him, Ray." And another, "Take him out."

"Did you just call me a tool?"

"What? You deaf or something?"

Troy hadn't planned for this. Leaving the boat, he had wanted to walk away from everything. Walk from Ray. From the desire to get even with him. From his tripping ego. That was empowerment.

Now, with Peter barking into Troy's ear, Ray pivoted on the stool and hurled a big fist. But it was telegraphed. And Troy ducked, making room for the blow to land on Peter's talking jaw, which stopped him midsentence as he ranted about Emma and how they were "mending the relationship."

Peter fell back and rubbed his chin, blood trickling from the corner of his mouth. Holy cow, Troy thought in astonishment, the preppie guy could take a punch.

Ray seemed perplexed. Then was apologetic, until Peter tackled him into the counter.

"Fight!" a burly bystander shouted.

Jimmy snatched his drink and stepped aside to avoid the brawl when the brutes hit the floor and started pounding on each other's faces.

Troy considered jumping in, but Peter seemed more than capable of handling Ray; so he slipped between the mob and found Emma standing by the jukebox. "Let's go," he said, leading her outside the tavern by the hand and into the snow-covered parking lot.

"You're crazy," Emma said excitedly. "Know that?"

"Who, me?"

They were laughing hard, puffs of steam shooting from their mouths.

"You're like the *Karate Kid.*"

"Just thought the Fireside needed a little pick-me-up."

"Oh my god, the way you ducked, and how Ray hit Peter, that was one of the funniest things I've ever seen." They ventured across the lot toward Emma's Chevy truck, a light snow falling. "I didn't know you were so athletic," she went on. "Have you ever played sports?"

"Yup."

"Really?"

She had no idea he played basketball, except for those pickup games with employees at her dad's warehouse. "I'll tell you about it sometime."

They stopped at the truck, black, new, her daddy's. "Thanks for getting me out of that stinky place," she said. "The smoke was burning my eyes."

"Mine too."

"Plus, I wanted to hang out with you."

"I was counting down the time to midnight."

She smiled.

It was cold, so they stood close and then somehow, while talking about going to a movie the next day, they found themselves embraced in each other's arms... and soon kissing.

Had she kissed first?

Or was it you?

He didn't know.

"Mmm," she muttered, pulling back. "I have to admit, I think about you all the time."

"You do?"

"Ever since last summer, when I first met you at my father's plant."

"I couldn't have guessed."

"It's true."

"I know how you feel. Because I—"

Patrons were stumbling from the tavern and into the parking lot. And there was Peter, disheveled and looking for Emma. "I don't want to see him right now," she said. "He's drunk. And he's jealous of you. Given what just happened. I should go."

"Okay." Troy opened the door for her. "So a movie? Tomorrow?"

"Can't wait. I get off at three."

"I'll meet you at the café."

A police car pulled into the parking lot with flashing lights. Troy wasn't worried. He hadn't thrown a single punch. And there were witnesses.

"Troy," she said. "I want to ask you something."

"Sure, what is it?"

"I heard, well, before you came to Alaska, that you spent time in jail? Not that it matters, but—"

"Who said that?"

"The rumors have been around. I don't know, it's just people talking."

"And what do they say?"

"That you killed someone."

Troy flinched. "It's true," he admitted. "But it was in self-defense. I got into some trouble and cut a deal with the Arizona district attorney to come here. And work. I've been on probation this entire time."

"I'm sorry, I shouldn't have—"

"It's alright. You need to know what's up."

Another police car rolled by.

112

Before climbing behind the wheel, Emma gave him a peck on the cheek. "Can't wait until tomorrow."

"Me neither."

With an insecure voice, she asked, "You won't blow me off, will you?"

"No. Never."

"My friends warned me."

"Oh?"

"Said I should stay away from guys like you."

"Really?"

"Or get my heart broken."

Troy smiled. "And what do you think?"

"I think it's worth the risk." Then she said goodbye, closed the door, and drove off.

Right away, with no intention of sticking around, Troy turned the other way and walked home.

Hours later, and dead asleep, Troy heard a rap rap rap on the door. *What the?* He eyed the alarm clock: it was 4:09 a.m.

"Hold on," he grumbled, rubbing his eyes. "I'm coming."

Walking to the door with a blanket over his shoulders, the apartment cold as an icebox, he figured it was Chloe showing up after a night of drinking and wanting to make up. He would have to level with her. She was gorgeous (probably the hottest girl he had ever been with) and genuinely a good person, but something was missing in their relationship. Besides, they argued over stupid things—his aloofness, his forgetfulness, how he hung out with Jimmy and his friends from the processing plant too much. When she drank, she often became angry and went off, sometimes punching him. They just weren't good for each other.

Troy opened the door and found a police officer staring at him.

"Troy Blake?" the officer asked.

"Hey, you got this wrong," Troy said defensively, his heart skipping. "I didn't have anything to do with that fight. Honest—"

The officer seemed confused. "I'm sorry," he interrupted, "but I have bad news."

"Oh? What is it?"

"Your brother." The cop wore a frown. "He's been killed."

Devastation.

And disbelief.

Troy was in so much shock he wasn't sure if he had even shed a tear. The police officer knew little of what happened, except that his brother had suffered a traumatic head injury.

Troy stayed awake. His phone was ringing off the hook, but he didn't answer. Didn't want to talk.

Couldn't talk.

The answering machine was full and couldn't accept more messages.

Off and on he thought about calling someone. His mom. Coach Chavez. Gabriela.

A few hours later, before taking the first flight to Anchorage, he swung by the diner to leave his cell number for Emma, along with a note stating he had a family emergency and was skipping town. He avoided the sad details. He'd explain later.

Troy handed the letter to a cashier named Beth, an older woman he didn't recognize, who said she would pass it along when Emma arrived for work later that morning.

"Are you okay?" Beth asked as he started away. "You look troubled."

Troy didn't respond. Instead, he went to the parking lot and took a taxicab to the Dutch Harbor airport.

The **Outlaw** Returns

"Billy was murdered," Chavez said. "Two days ago. After school. He was just shooting around on the family basketball court when someone confronted him."

"Was it gang related?"

"We don't know."

"A robbery?"

"It's unclear what happened. Or why."

Troy sat in the back seat of a Toyota Camry, taking the long Uber drive to Douglas. He was talking on the new iPhone he had purchased before leaving Tucson, where he'd spent the night after flying down from Anchorage.

"And what?" Though hard to find the words, he had to ask, "Billy was shot?"

"No." Troy sensed Chavez was uncomfortable talking about what happened. "Beat up."

It felt like a slug to the stomach. His little brother beat to death? The horrific moment when he struck José across the head with a bat sprang to mind. There was such a thing as getting even. "How could they do this?"

"They?"

"The Macho Boys."

"Troy, don't jump to conclusions. There's no evidence those punks had anything to do with the murder."

"I'll be the judge of that."

"The police have launched an investigation," Chavez explained. "They'll get to the bottom of everything."

Troy squeezed a fist. The long flight home had offered plenty of time for reflection. Could he have done something to prevent this? The question tore him apart. Yes. No. Maybe. Rubbing his forehead, he asked, "So what then? What's next?"

"We wait."

"Wait?" It sounded like a weak game plan. "Wait for what?"

"For justice."

Troy felt doubtful. There must be tons of unsolved murders in the Arizona cold case files. Many at the hands of cartels and border gangs.

Chavez continued, "As you might imagine, this has hit your mother hard."

"For sure."

"Have you spoken to her?"

"No. Just texted."

"Did she tell you there's a memorial service on Sunday?"

"Yup."

"Okay, good." Chavez probably knew what he was thinking because he added, "Your mother misses you."

"I know."

"She told me you haven't called in months."

"Well, I've been kind of busy."

"I understand. But call her, okay?"

"Sure, Coach."

"So, where are you headed now?"

"Home."

"To your house?" Chavez asked with alarm.

"Yes. Why do you seem so surprised?"

The coach gave a sound of exasperation. "She didn't tell you?"

"Tell me what?"

"There was a fire. Whoever assaulted your brother also torched the house."

"You mean?"

Troy hung up the phone, his heart racing and panic setting in. A fire? He had to see it for himself.

Minutes later, the Camry pulled onto a dirt road, driving up a desert hill and around a bend to reveal the destruction: the charred, black timbers of what was once his family home.

When the car came to a stop in front of the burned down house, the Uber driver asked, "Is this where you live?"

"Uh, yeah," Troy mumbled, stepping from the car with a duffle bag. "Something like that."

"Sorry, bro. You need a lift somewhere else?"

"No. I'm good."

The Camry drove off, leaving a trail of dust as it sped across the desolate road.

It was a sunny forty-seven degrees.

Troy dropped the bag on the basketball court and heaved a sigh. Was this really happening? He walked past his parked Ford truck, covered in mud from Billy's four-wheeling, and stepped into the black debris where the living room used to be. *Charred timbers now.* Then he moved down the remnants of a hallway and into the relics of his former bedroom.

Gone.

Everything.

Sadly, he recognized bits and pieces of what used to be his bed, a dresser, and a chair. A section of plastic CRIME SCENE tape was caught in the fragments. He shook his head in disbelief. The things he had collected as a kid: the autographed Steve Nash poster, the baseball card collection, and the Phoenix Suns memorabilia. Everything had been destroyed in the fire.

He sifted through the wreckage, pushing away timbers, kicking over the box spring, until he found a fire-resistant safe about the size of a shoebox. Cradling the metal container, he returned to the truck and placed it in the passenger footwell. The safe, which he had purchased at Home Depot, was more like a king's treasure chest. Steve Nash poster aside, its contents were the only items worth saving.

Brushing the ash from his hands, he climbed into the jacked-up truck and sped away.

Crazy, less than forty-eight hours ago he was standing in a foot of Alaskan snow, wearing a heavy jacket and gloves, and planning a fun date with Emma. Now this.

He groaned.

With his life in a nosedive, his love for Emma was the only thing keeping him from collapsing just then. He grabbed the iPhone and called the diner in Dutch Harbor and spoke to a woman named Alice.

"What do you mean Emma quit?" he said.

"When you blew her off," Alice replied. "She was really upset and went home."

It sickened him. That he had let her down. And exactly as she had feared. "I didn't mean to," he explained, turning onto the highway toward downtown Douglas. "But something came up. A family crisis. I needed to catch the first plane out. I left a note. Did she get it?"

"A note?"

"I gave it to Beth."

"Hold on a sec," Alice replied. Troy waited on the phone for about five minutes, speeding past slow cars, his knuckles turning red on the wheel. What gives? How hard is it to pass along a note? The woman came back, "You still there, Troy?"

"Yup."

"Beth said she gave the message to Emma."

"Oh, good."

"Look ..." Alice wasn't the friendliest café employee, and now it seemed like she was playing defense when she explained that Emma was leaving town in the next day or so for her sophomore year. "And she's back together with Peter," she declared. "I'd advise you to leave the girl alone. She's not interested in you."

"But we talked the other night. They were broken up—"

"You seem like a nice guy. So, I hate to tell you this, but Peter has a college degree. He's a manager. He's going places."

"But—"

"Goodbye, Troy."

He banged a fist on the steering wheel. It was his own fault. In the note, his "goodbye" words were heartfelt, though vague; he should have explained what happened to his brother, why he had left Dutch Harbor so unexpectedly. Emma must think he blew her off or something.

His head felt like it would explode. Things were happening too fast. Troy leaned back in the seat and let out a deep breath.

You got to take this one day at a time.

One day.

Everything will work itself out.

He drove to the Douglas Walmart Supercenter and climbed from the truck. It had warmed up, so he took off the hoodie to reveal a white and orange Phoenix Suns jersey—Steve Nash, number thirteen.

For no reason except that he wasn't feeling very social, Troy didn't want anyone to know he was in town. He was planning to stay just long enough to attend Billy's service and then maybe visit with friends for a day or two before hitting the road. Putting an Arizona Diamondbacks cap on backwards, he hoped to hide behind dark sunglasses and a woodsman beard.

He found a blue shopping cart and pushed it into the busy store.

After browsing through the video games, he made his way to the

Outdoors section of the store and grabbed a large tent and some camping gear, including a sleeping bag and kerosene lamp.

In the next few aisles, he picked up a plastic cooler and a garden hose.

Before wheeling his way to the checkout lines, he went to the grocery aisles and loaded up with a case of bottled water and some snacks.

Ready to make his purchase, he waited in line behind a woman with coupons and a family with two carts full of stuff. Whipping out his iPhone, he surfed to ESPN, before looking up the Arizona Southern basketball schedule. When it was his turn to pay, the male cashier, having scanned most of his items, burst out excitedly, "Hey, aren't you Troy Blake?"

It caught him off guard. "You recognize me?"

"Not with the beard." The young cashier's eyes grew wide, a starstruck fan. He was maybe eighteen, with a buzz cut and a silver hoop pierced through an eyebrow. "The skull and snake tattoo on your shoulder gave you away."

"Oh, I see."

"I used to watch you play basketball at the old YMCA. You were awesome, dude. Kicked some serious ass."

Troy nodded. "That's how we played."

"They called you the 'Outlaw,' right?"

"Yup."

"Well, you're sort of infamous these days."

"Infamous?"

"You know: insane baller. Notorious killer."

"Killer. You mean—"

"The way you took out that freakazoid who called himself the The Big Crusher."

"Umm ... nothing I'm proud of."

The cashier apparently didn't pick up on the self-reflection in his reply. Or the apologetic attitude. "The gang members tied you to a basketball hoop, right?"

"Like a damn dog."

"Jerks."

"I don't know what their problem was with me."

"Well, you're the real deal," the cashier said. "Guys still talk about you. And those epic cage battles."

"Mmm... those were the best of times," Troy said distantly.

The cashier smiled. "You're the greatest thing that ever happened in this lousy town."

"Really? Why do you say that?"

"Because you gave us something to be excited about. How you ripped it up at Arizona Southern. And crushed it in the cage. You showed people in the big cities that hoopsters in Douglas are big-time, too."

Troy glanced over his shoulder. A Mexican father wore a "hurry the hell up" expression while his kids jumped around him. The man could care less about Troy's glory days, the baller formally known as The Outlaw, or his success as a JUCO player.

"Guys remember me, huh?"

"In an epic way, dude."

Like an addict drawing up heroin, Troy craved the attention. "Yo, I don't know about 'epic,' but if you say people still remember me, that's cool."

After scanning the rest of the items, the cashier asked, "So, what's the deal? Are you going to play in the cage again?"

It hit him hard—he really wanted to play. "No."

"Why not?"

"Because I'm done with it."

"Done?"

"Retired."

And yet he wondered: did the League still exist? A few months ago, maybe the last time he talked to Diego, he learned the cage had been torn down and the YMCA boarded up after the city finally condemned the building.

"Ah, too bad." Handing Troy the receipt, the cashier added, "Anyway, sorry about what happened to your little brother."

"Yeah, thanks."

"He had the sweetest shot." A frown replaced the excitement. "Billy could've been All-American."

"No doubt."

"Take care, Mr. Infamous."

Troy nodded. "Later, bro."

He pushed the blue cart across the parking lot. So much for relying on the beard and shades for incognito status. Next time, he would hide the tattoos with a long-sleeved shirt.

He placed the camping gear and groceries into the truck's scratched-up bed. The plan was to pitch a tent beside the family basketball court and camp for a few days. It might seem strange, especially to the neighbors, but sleeping in the desert was more his style—even sleeping next to his burned down home. Thanks to the lucrative fishing industry, Troy had $38,000 in his savings account. He could easily afford the luxury of a Best Western; however, right now he wanted to avoid people. Friends, strangers, even motel staff.

He reached into his pocket for the keys but froze when a white school bus rolled to a stop in the parking lot. Painted on the side was a rock star Jesus Christ jamming on an electric guitar. The words METAL CHURCH BUS adorned its side.

The door abruptly swung open. "Need a lift, brother?" the driver yelled over a blast of Iron Maiden playing on the radio.

"Huh?"

"To the next destination."

Troy gave the holy rocker a closer look. He had long, graying hair and wore a leather vest, pants, and spiked gloves. He was maybe in his late fifties with a wisp of hair beneath his lower lip.

"Uh, I think you got the wrong guy."

The driver smiled. "No, brother. You are the one."

"Me?" It felt weird, but somehow, he couldn't turn away.

"Allow me to introduce myself," the rocker said theatrically, "the name's Peavey. I am the Pastor of the new rock and roll church in town. Former roadie for Judas Priest, now doing penance for years of the Triple D."

"Triple what?"

"Drugs, drinking, and debauchery."

"Oh, I see."

"This Church bus offers free daily rides to and fro Mexico. Even around town if ya like."

"Well, I don't need a lift."

"Mmm …" he winkled, "then again, you never know. You just might someday."

"Okay. Cool. Thanks."

Peavey's vest was covered in patches, everything from Motörhead's war pig to the Rolling Stones tongue. "Anyway, driving by just now, I had this strangest of strange feelings. Don't exactly know what it's about, but I sense you have important work to do. God's work."

"God's work?" Troy couldn't help but repeat the words. What a dumb thing to say. "Uh, I just came to Walmart for a few things. You must be mistaken."

Peavey smiled reassuringly. "Rock on, brother. And God will give you strength."

"Okay, whatever you say," Troy replied, offering a friendly wave as the bus rolled off, the sound of heavy metal thrashing across the parking lot.

Driving home, with the barren hills and desert brush framing a vast Mad Max-like wasteland on either side of the highway, he thought about the heavy metal Jesus freak and his prophecy. *God's work.*

Was it God's work when he roughed up that baller from Inglewood back in the day? Hardly. His name was Willie Michael Dee, but he called himself "WMD." Troy's sixth and bloodiest cage victim. The guy was a former high school basketball legend who wore a maroon jersey with number fifteen. A beast; with veins snaking across his shaved head. He was on parole for armed robbery or something. Word leading up to the game was that WMD talked a lot of trash about how Troy was a "bitch ass white boy" and made threats about how he was going to "pulverize The Outlaw" before entering the cage to N.W.A's *Gangsta Gangsta*.

It wasn't even close.

Final score: Outlaw 68, WMD 51—the third time Troy had scored 60 points in the cage.

Troy's phone dinged and buzzed, tugging him from the memory. He was getting text messages left and right. Everyone wanted to make sure he was okay. His mom. Gabriela. Diego. Jackson. Coach Chavez.

Really, it was too much.

That night, a cool Sonoran breeze slapped against the tent. Nocturnal critters, coyotes, rattlesnakes, and scorpions lurked beneath the stars.

Troy sat on a sleeping bag, his tired eyes glued to the iPhone while reading about his brother's murder. Among the theories published in local news was that it had been a botched robbery. The Blake home was located in a remote desert community of mostly unsold lots and older ranch homes on acreage. The neighborhood had experienced a record number of border-related crimes in recent years. Without any suspects, it was the most obvious explanation of what had happened; nevertheless, other ideas spun in the tornado ripping through Troy's brain. For one thing, the murder just so happened to take place on the eve of his probation coming to an end. Even though Chavez had dismissed the theory, Troy suspected Juan Carlos was behind the beating. Wasn't it obvious, a vendetta?

He scrolled through dozens of text messages he had missed in recent weeks, from mom, from Chavez, from friends, from Billy. He paused to read where his brother had shared the exiting recruitment news,

I'M TAKING MY TALENTS TO NEVADA

Without a cell phone, Troy hadn't responded to the good news. And so, he thought regretfully, the silence must have been a bummer. Even a simple "congratulations" or "way to go" would have showed his brother some love. Instead, he got what, rejection? Troy set aside the iPhone. Like haunting words from the grave, Billy's text messages were too difficult to read.

He crawled over to the fireproof safe and entered the lock's combination.

Inside, basking in the lantern light, his father's service medals gleamed like King Solomon's lost treasure.

There was the 1963 Pete Rose rookie baseball card his grandfather had given him.

Scholarship offers from several Top 25 basketball schools.

Letters from the war.

His father's Glock pistol.

And a few bullets.

Though it was illegal in Arizona to own a handgun until he was twenty-one, Troy placed the weapon next to his sleeping bag and watched SportsCenter on YouTube TV.

Now wasn't the time to be concerned about the law.

A STEADY vibrating.

It was cold. Maybe thirty-some degrees in the tent. He rolled in the sleeping bag until he found the iPhone and half asleep answered, "Hello?"

"Troy Blake?"

"Yes, sir."

"This is Sergeant Stanley Jones. I'm with the Douglas Police Department. Sorry to bother you so early in the morning, but it's with respect to your brother." Now he jolted awake. Had they found the killer? "If possible, I'd like to meet with you today," Jones added. "Are you available at ten o'clock?"

"Uh, this morning?"

"Yes."

"Sure," Troy replied. Anything for justice.

He arrived at the police station a few minutes before ten. He wore a black flannel shirt to cover the tattoos, and the Diamondbacks hat that, combined with his scraggly beard, made him look like a cross between a young Waylon Jennings and a hobo.

He was led to an office at the back of the building, passing by doors marked with words like SPECIAL INVESTIGATION and CRIME SCENE SECTION and UNIT SIX.

Sgt. Jones greeted him with a firm handshake and a nod. He was a fit, middle-aged man with a graying horseshoe mustache. Give the guy an Old West costume and a pair of six-shooters, and he could easily play the part of a gunslinger during Tombstone's Wyatt Earp Days.

Jones promptly congratulated him on successfully serving out the probation. "Well done," he said, his upbeat tone feeling like a high-five. "The Department was pulling for you. Every step of the way."

Inviting Troy to have a seat, the police officer expressed his sorrow for Billy, for what had happened to his father in Afghanistan, and asked how his mother was holding up. He seemed genuinely concerned.

In response, Troy offered basic answers— "She's good," and, "We'll get through this"— before asking the man about his brother's murder.

"The murder," Jones said despondently, shaking his head, "has torn this community apart." Surprisingly, twenty minutes since entering the office, Jones hadn't offered much information on the case, aside from the scant details Troy already knew: that his brother was assaulted on the family's basketball court and that there weren't any suspects. "But keep the faith," Jones added, "I'm confident our investigation will lead to an arrest."

"It doesn't sound like you have many leads."

"Between the fire," Jones said, "and a winter storm that blew through the day he was killed, the crime scene was essentially destroyed before forensic experts could examine the area for evidence like footprints, hair follicles, and blood DNA."

Troy leaned back in the chair. Why had Jones wanted to meet? What was the point to this? Focusing on his own investigation, he asked, "What about The Macho Boys?"

"What about them?"

"Well, if you want my honest opinion, those losers should be tops on your list of suspects."

Jones lit a cigarette and took a long draw. "I understand why you see things that way," he replied. "Really, I wish I could lock them up. All of 'em. They are the source of a lot of petty crime this side of the border. However, other than the beef you had with..."

The police officer was struggling to remember the gang leader's name, so Troy filled in the blank. "Juan. His name is Juan."

"Yes, Juan Carlos."

"And?"

"We have nothing on him or his goons that suggests they might be involved in this particular crime."

Troy cracked his knuckles and groaned. The officer seemed legit but was operating way too much by the book. "I did kill his cousin in self-defense."

"True."

"I'm sure he hasn't forgotten."

"No. I'm sure he hasn't."

"So maybe he or one of his gang members killed Billy as payback."

Jones blew smoke. "Look, anything is possible. However, we can't make arrests based upon speculation."

"Just offering my two cents."

"Though, speaking of The Macho Boys," Jones locked onto Troy's eyes, "the main reason I wanted you to come down to the station this morning is because word has gotten out."

"Word? What word?"

Jones tamped out the cigarette. "That you've come home."

"And?"

"And I'd advise you to keep it cool. Stay away from basketball courts and other public places. Especially around Agua Prieta. You have no business over there."

Troy shrugged. "But I've done nothing wrong."

"No, you haven't."

"Then what's up? What do I have to be so worried about?"

Jones pitched the coffee cup into the trashcan. "We have informants on the streets. And word is, if you cross the border to Mexico, well, we can't protect you over there."

"I wouldn't expect you to."

"There's a bounty on your head in Mexico. Compliments of Los Niños Machos. One hundred grand to whoever kills you."

"A hundred grand?"

"Yup."

Troy considered the advice. He had heard of people getting into trouble on the Mexican side—the hellish prison cells some were thrown into, unmarked graves for others—but there were too many unanswered questions, and the police didn't have any solid leads. Bounty or no bounty, nothing mattered except the pursuit of truth. And, he thought next, maybe vigilante justice.

"A hundred grand?" Troy said sarcastically. "Really? That all I'm worth?"

Jones snickered. He wasn't impressed with Troy's fearless attitude. "Look, it's simple. We don't need another dead Blake kid on our hands."

Troy flipped his hat backwards and left the office in a whirl of confusion, fist bumping a young cop on the way out the door.

Another dead Blake. That was a heartless thing for Sgt. Jones to say. Was he trying to scare him? Probably. But was he being truthful about the hundred grand? Most likely.

Troy climbed into the truck, reached his hand into the glove compartment, and felt for the handgun. It didn't matter. He could fend for himself. His dad had raised him to be self-reliant, a one-man army, a survivalist if need be. So long as he had his dad's loaded Glock, he wasn't afraid of Juan Carlos or any of his Mexican clowns.

He pulled away from the parking lot and headed toward the college.

Along the way, the Metal Church Bus approached from the opposite lane. Heavy drums and energetic guitar music blasted through the open windows. Peavey, in leather and sunglasses, offered a friendly beep on the horn and a devil horns hand gesture. That song—Metallica, was it? Passing the bus, Troy turned and looked over his shoulder. A sign in the rear window read:

FOR I DO NOT DO THE GOOD I WANT, BUT THE
EVIL I DO NOT WANT IS WHAT I KEEP DOING

ROMANS 7:19

Troy stopped by the gymnasium. The Scorpions had a home game that night. Chavez, a consummate X's and O's guy, was in his office watching film of the opposing team. Pausing the video, the coach stood and gave Troy a hug.

"I'm sorry," he said, before sharing his grief for Billy. Ten minutes into the conversation, the teary-eyed coach realized that Troy didn't want to talk about his brother's death and returned to the swivel chair. But added, "So you're hanging tough?"

"I'm alright."

"Good. Okay."

"Given everything that's happened."

"Anytime you want to talk, let me know. I'm always here for you."

"Thanks, Coach."

Chavez was drinking a Coke. "Then what's up, my man? It hasn't been the same without you around here."

"You mean with the wins situation?"

"Yeah, that, too," Chavez groaned, obviously stewing over the team's losing record. "Are you coming to tonight's game? I have a free ticket. We could use a little Troy Blake luck in the bleachers."

"Naw, don't think so," Troy replied, gripping the backpack strap slung over his shoulder. "I'm not feeling very social these days."

"I understand."

"Besides," he went on, "to be honest with you, Coach, since I'm not on the team, it kind of depresses me to watch the guys hoop it up."

"Naturally," Chavez replied. "You're a competitor. The fire never goes away. In fact, not a day passes when I don't wish I was out there on the court. Even in my dreams, I can slam the ball."

"But you never could slam, could you?"

Chavez cracked a smile. "No. Only in my dreams."

Troy nodded in jest. "Keep at it, Coach."

"But seriously," Chavez insisted, "anytime you want to talk about a fresh start, whether it's here at Arizona Southern, or someplace else, you come see me."

"Actually..." Troy reached into his backpack and pulled out the blue folder that contained the college entrance paperwork he had been working on. "Actually, that's why I'm here."

"Oh?"

"I have a small favor to ask."

"Sure. Anything. What is it?"

"Well, if you still believe in me, I need a letter of recommendation."

THE COMFORTS of a Motel 6 were looking more and more like the better way to go. Camping was cool and everything, but Troy's body was stiff from sleeping on an air mattress and the desert nights were super cold. Taking an icy morning shower in the front yard with a rubber garden hose wasn't his favorite thing, either; and swearing through the agonizing ordeal didn't help much.

Drying off, he threw on jeans, a black, long sleeve Under Armour shirt, and pulled over the Steve Nash jersey. He tucked the loaded Glock into a bellyband behind his pants and covered it with the hoops shirt. Wearing army-style boots he dug the keys from his pocket and walked toward the truck.

More and more, his brother's death seemed like a premeditated hit instead of some random act of border violence. Billy was killed during the day. Drug runners, Troy's *Crime Scene Investigation* state of mind made the case, typically crossed the border at night—and in a more remote location than the outskirts of Douglas. He respected the police, especially Sergeant Jones, but felt the investigation, despite any good intentions, was heading down the wrong path. Like he had attempted to explain to Chavez and whoever else would listen, the murder reeked of revenge. It had to be the work of The Macho Boys. The hundred grand on his head was reason enough to believe this theory.

As he opened the door, something gleaming in the sunlight caught his attention. A piece of glass? He walked to the front of the truck and leaned over. It was a shattered bottle of Pepe Sanchez brand tequila. Strange. No one drank that crap in his family. None of his friends did, either. He moved the glass with the tip of his boot before climbing into the truck and peeling away.

When he reached the highway, he dialed up Jimmy, keeping one hand on the steering wheel and the other hand holding the phone to his ear. When his Cajun friend answered, Troy said, "What's up, seadog?"

"Well, hot damn, how are you, Troy?"

"I'm in Arizona."

"Arizona? I was wondering what happened to you."

Jimmy's voice thundered with excitement until he learned why Troy had bolted from Dutch Harbor so unexpectedly. Without getting into the gut-wrenching details, Troy wanted to get word to the captain that he was leaving the boat due to his brother's death. "I left a message," Troy explained. "But Radanovich never calls back."

"Yup, I know."

"Anyway, I'll try calling him again when things calm down."

"Take care of your personal business," Jimmy said. "Don't worry about the captain. He will always have you back on his crew. You were the hardest working mate on the boat. After me, of course."

"Thanks Jimmy."

"Well, I'm sorry to hear about your brother."

"I'll get through it. Somehow."

"You stay in touch."

"I will."

"And hey, let me know when you go back to school and play basketball again."

Hanging up, Troy drove toward an old chapel and cemetery near his home. A garden of cactus and Palo Verde trees surrounded the sacred grounds.

Hidden behind the scruffy beard and sunglasses, he entered the adobe chapel, a small, white structure built sometime in the late 1800s by a Jesuit missionary. About fifty people, most of them wearing black, had gathered inside the space: family, friends, a few kids from school, everyone waiting for his brother's service to begin. He spotted Billy's casket at the lectern and felt a chill looking at the rows of sports trophies resting on the lid—the awards obviously donations from friends since the originals had burned in the fire.

A tear welled up, but he fought it back.

Surprisingly, no one recognized him. In fact, standing by himself, with his hands in his pockets, he felt like a stranger at the private family ceremony. It wasn't only his beard, or his resemblance to a young country music star; rather, he felt eerily out of place. In the loneliness, he missed Alaska and oddly longed for the hazardous days aboard *Romanov II*. Especially the way Radanovich had whipped the crew into shape.

Very few people would understand.

He had confronted the ocean.

He had experienced sleepless nights for days on end.

He had fallen overboard and nearly drowned.

The trials aboard the fishing boat had shed new light on his world. Now he believed there was more to life than the senseless troubles of a border town.

An Asian woman stroked a cello at the front of the room while people spoke softly.

Diego and Gabriela stood in the main aisle. Looking closer he saw they were holding hands. What the—? He approached but didn't interrupt their conversation until his friend turned to him in surprise and said, "Troy?"

"Yup."

"Wow, I didn't recognize you with that beard."

Gabriela shouted his name excitedly, and then threw her arms around his shoulders for a hug. "I'm so sorry," she said with glassy eyes. "I loved Billy like a brother."

"I know you did."

"I still can't believe he's gone."

"Me neither."

After a somber moment, Diego asked, "When did you get back?"

"Yesterday."

Troy and Diego did their ritual shake, though their motions were somewhat subdued. "Looks like," Troy began, noticing the ring on Gabriela's finger, "the two of you are what … together?"

"We're engaged," Diego said. "We wanted to tell you in person."

"Engaged? For real?"

"Yes."

Troy patted Diego on the shoulder. "Oh, that's awesome," he said, sensing their anxiety about his reaction, especially considering he and Gabriela had dated in high school. But it was good news. It really was. He was happy for them. Somehow, the announcement lightened his mood.

"You okay with it?" Diego asked.

"Of course, bro." A pause. "I always knew you were meant for each other."

"You're too sweet," Gabriela said.

"And I want you to be my best man," Diego added. "You're my first and only choice."

"For sure," Troy replied.

"So," Gabriela changed the subject with a somber voice, "this is difficult. But how are you holding up?"

Troy felt the lingering sickness in his stomach. That endless, dark pit of depression that threatened to bring him to his knees. "I don't know, doesn't seem real," he replied, his sad eyes hidden behind the sunglasses. What else could he say? "Blows my mind. I mean…

Billy. Why him?"

Gabriela wiped a tear from her cheek. "I just had lunch with him last week."

Troy moaned at a surge of emotion. It was easier to block out what had happened. Pretend this was just a dream. Kick it around the corner. Anything than face reality. His face grew taut like a war drum, lips tight and stern.

Soon, Jackson and a few players from Billy's basketball team gathered around, releasing him from the torment and suffering. They offered their sympathies, expressing how awesome Billy was as a friend and team player. The conversation eventually turned to Troy and his year away in Alaska, and he was bombarded with questions about what it was like being on a crab boat.

"Is it really like that TV show *The Deadliest Catch*?"

"Yeah, sure," Troy mumbled, not really wanting to get into it. In some ways the experience was; though mostly, fishing wasn't as exciting as the show made it seem.

"Cool, well, when things settle down, let's find some time to hoop it up," Jackson injected, sporting a big afro. He had gained muscle and was looking incredibly fit. From what Troy read online, he was the best player on the last place Scorpions. This alone, Troy thought cynically, would explain their losing record.

"I'm in."

"One-on-one after practice," Jackson added, his girlfriend standing next to him.

"Yeah, let's do it," Troy replied with little enthusiasm.

"Judging by how out of shape you look," Jackson went on, "I'll spot you ten points." He ran his hand across Troy's stomach and flashed a mocking smile. "What they feeding you in Alaska, homey?"

Troy huffed. Then with a friendly voice, spat back, "You versus me. Any day, buddy."

It was only when he finally spotted his mother that he felt

himself choke up and wiped a tear from his eye. "Remember to stay strong," an inner voice spoke out. "Find the guy who murdered your brother. Tears are a sign of weakness." With muscles in his neck stretching tight, and drying eyes, he knocked Jackson on the shoulder and excused himself. "Later, dude."

"I really missed you," Linda Blake said, embracing her son with a snivel.

"Hang in there, Mom."

Between sobs, she expressed her sorrow, her devastation for a world falling apart, though much of what she said wasn't particularly coherent. Probably because he smelled booze on her breath. Eventually, her unhappiness seemed to temporarily lift from her shoulders, and she said, "You look so much older with that beard."

"Really?" He shrugged. "I guess ..."

Leaning back, and scanning him from head to toe, she added, "And you look a little meaty. I like it."

"Okay, Mom, enough about my appearance."

"You've always been so skinny."

"Mom," he protested, "it's called zero body fat. It's what athletes strive for." Truth was, it annoyed him how everyone kept mentioning how out of shape he was.

Next, he shook hands with Larry but couldn't stomach looking the pothead in the eye. The man reeked of marijuana. Or maybe it was his cheap cologne. Troy gave his mother's boyfriend a pass and talked to him for a few minutes about life on the fishing boat, before the guy mentioned he had tickets to see the 80s soft rock band Air Supply. "It's going to be a sweet concert," he said. "Want to come with?"

"Uh, think I'll take a rain check," Troy replied. "But thanks anyway."

Soon his mother mentioned she was planning a larger ceremony at Billy's high school, where she hoped Troy, along with several other friends, would pay special tribute to his brother. "It'll take place next month," she added. "The school is going to name a seat in the gym's bleachers in his honor."

"Cool."

"But I'll tell you more later." She paused. "By now you must know about the house fire?"

"I saw."

"After today's service, we're heading up to Phoenix to meet with the insurance company."

"Hope it goes well."

As the priest called for everyone to sit, she added quickly, "I was going to tell you about the fire, but I didn't want to stress you out."

"It's all good."

"Do you want to come with us? You know, and hang out in Phoenix?"

"No, thanks."

"How about dinner before we leave?"

"Let's wait until you get back," Troy said, pulling a wad of cash from his pocket—five thousand dollars in hundred-dollar bills—and placing the money in the palm of her hand.

"What's this?" she asked, her eyes suddenly sober.

"A Christmas gift. Sorry it's late."

"I can't take this money."

"Sure you can."

"You worked hard for it."

"Please. Keep it, Mom."

"But Troy—"

He hugged his mother before walking to the front of the room and sat in a pew beside Coach Chavez, his friends surrounding him.

After the service, he snuck away from the crowd and sped into the hills east of Douglas Municipal Airport. He parked on the side of the road, hopped over a barricade, walked down a short trail, and then climbed onto a mound of boulders and small rocks. Holding the gun, he gazed across the border toward the Mexican town of Agua Prieta.

Questions stirred. The murder. The killer. The reason. Did the answers lie in Mexico?

Probably.

Did he care about the price on his head?

No.

He would do anything for his brother.

The shattered bottle of Pepe Sanchez was on his mind, too. No one drank that brand of tequila in his family. He was pretty sure Larry didn't either—Larry pretty much hated Mexicans and anything to do with Mexico.

Something didn't add up.

A text message from Diego suddenly appeared on his phone:

DUDE, LET'S HOOP IT UP. TOMORROW. YOUR CAMPSITE.

Troy responded with a thumbs-up emoji.

TROY'S SHOT rattled around the rim and fell into Diego's swiping hands. Another bad miss. Another hustle rebound for his best friend.

Playing one-on-one in the glow of the truck's headlights, *Down with the Sickness* by Disturbed on the stereo, Troy was surprised how out of shape he was.

Now dribbling across the faded 3-point line, officially bringing it back, Diego made room with his forearm and drove for a slashing layup, sliding his shooting hand beneath Troy's outstretched arms and letting the ball roll off his fingertips. The ball kissed the backboard and slipped through the net.

Troy put his hands on his head to catch his breath. It was 42 degrees but playing hard made it feel more like ninety.

"Game," Diego said, smiling over the unexpected victory.

"Whatever," Troy replied cynically, looking down on Diego who was five inches shorter. He was upset with himself, with his sad, sad basketball skills. Exactly how far had he fallen? He walked to the faucet and drank water from the rubber hose.

"Haven't been playing, have you?" Diego asked.

"Who, me? No. I've been sticking my freaking hands in fish goo. Freezing my ass off in the Bearing Sea. What'd you think?"

"Just joking."

"Funny."

"First time I've ever beat you."

"Congratulations." Troy retied one of his shoes.

"I didn't mean it like that."

Just then headlights appeared on the dirt road leading to the campsite. Troy's mind reacted, Macho Boys? Racing to the tent, he grabbed the handgun from beneath a pillow. "This is your turf," he whispered. "Defend it." Locked and loaded, he returned to the basketball court fully prepared to fire the weapon.

"Dude, relax," Diego blurted. "It's just Gabriela."

A white Jeep Wrangler stopped next to Troy's truck. Gabriela climbed from the vehicle with a box of Big Pig's Pizza and stepped into the 4x4's bright lights. Her face washed in concern, dark eyes narrowing in on the gun's muzzle, she seemed more "what-the-hell are you doing?" than frightened by the weapon.

"Seriously?" she asked.

"My bad," Troy replied, lowering the Glock. "Thought you were Juan Carlos."

"Better control that paranoia."

"Whatever." Troy snickered, walking toward the bonfire.

"Anyway," she persisted, "why do you have that stupid thing in the first place?"

"Just exercising my second amendment rights."

Gabriela looked at Diego. "What's the deal?" she asked. "Did you beat him in basketball or something?"

"It was a close game," Diego said apologetically.

Gabriela chased after Troy. When she opened her mouth again, it felt like mom shouting into his ear, her voice shrill. "Hey," she persisted, "you aren't allowed to own a handgun in Arizona. You're not twenty-one."

"Ah, don't worry about it."

"I am worried. You could get into serious trouble."

"Besides, it's not my gun." He smirked. "I don't own it. The gun belongs to my father."

"Yeah, so I'm pretty sure that's not the way the law works." Gabriela shook her head, before giving up the quasi interrogation.

Sitting around the fire, they passed the pizza box. Troy had calmed down. But he didn't feel like talking so kept to himself. He felt incredibly agitated and was acting like a sore loser. It wasn't just the whooping at Diego's hands that had him freaking mad at the world. Or Gabriela's motherly scolding. There was a deep, out-of-control burn in the pit of his stomach.

Stay strong.

Control your anger, he thought, the gun resting by his shoe.

Find the killer.

For a moment, during the pick-up game, after Diego had hacked him on the wrist, he had wanted to push back. For no legit reason, he wanted to punch his friend in the face. Inflict some pain.

"Arizona Southern has a good Phys Ed program," Diego was saying.

"Huh?"

"Our school."

"Oh."

"Coach said maybe you can get your scholarship back. Join the team. Work on your degree."

Troy shrugged, annoyed. "I don't ball anymore."

"Done with it?"

"Yup."

"I find that hard to believe."

"Well, believe." Troy grabbed a packet of chili peppers and sprinkled the contents over his slice of pepperoni. Then popping open a Corona, he added, "But hey, I got a question for you. What's up with Miguel Ángel these days?"

Diego replied, "Miguel?"

"Yes, where is he?"

"Don't know. Haven't seen him. Why?"

"Just wondering."

Gabriela weighed in, "The Macho Boys are still dodging questions about what happened last year."

Troy raised an eyebrow. He assumed that meant Mexican authorities had refused to extradite Juan and his gang members to the U.S. for questioning. "So, what then? He's hiding in Mexico?"

"Yup. Probably living with his aunt."

"And he's still a member of the Wuss Boys?"

"I guess. I mean—" Gabriela cleared her throat. What was she about to say? "I haven't spoken to him in months." It sounded like she was trying to change the topic. "Things got pretty bad after you left. You know, the hate. The them versus us thing."

"Why are you asking?" Diego inquired.

"I have a few questions."

"Oh?"

"About Billy."

Diego grabbed a slice of pizza, and said, "I'm pretty sure he doesn't want to talk to you anymore. So maybe best to —"

"I'm interested in what he's heard on the streets," Troy snapped. "That's all."

141

"Well, if it's about Billy, maybe we can answer the questions."

When Diego looked uneasily toward Gabriela, it raised the red flags in Troy's head. Their strange behavior. The way they dodged his questions. Why were they being so evasive?

"Let me ask you something." Troy zeroed in on Diego's eyes. "Do you like Pepe Sanchez tequila?"

"I don't drink."

"Well, do you know anyone who does?"

"None that I can think of. Why?"

"Because I found a shattered bottle of Pepe Sanchez the other day. Right over there." He pointed toward darkness. "By where the front door used to be."

"So?"

"So I happen to know Juan and his little d-bags drink that crap."

"And what, you think —"

"I think he was here." Troy's face was grim. "I think he was here the day Billy died." He let the statement sink in, taking a swig of beer, and feeling the urge to punch his best friend, because, after all, it seemed like he was lying about something.

"I seriously doubt it. He wouldn't risk stepping foot in the U.S."

"Oh, says who?"

"None of them would." Diego frowned. "Like Gabby said, the cops have questions."

"Yeah, well, so do I."

"Your imagination is out of control, bro. You better get rid of those dangerous thoughts."

"That's right," Gabriela blurted, "you shouldn't stir up any trouble with Juan. Let it go. He's bad news."

Troy shook his head. Two against one. His friends were a legit one-two punch. Lunging, he grabbed Diego by the shirt collar. "What the hell, man? I know when you're being real and when you're being a dick. What are you hiding from me?"

"Dude, relax." Diego pulled away, the slice of pizza falling into his lap. "Stop acting like a jerk."

"C'mon," Gabriela intervened. "Take it easy, guys."

Whatever was eating her up, some dark little secret, maybe the real scoop on Miguel, was unleashed with a huge breath. "Troy's right," she said. "We can't keep this from him any longer."

"Keep what from me?"

"Look, we we're just trying to protect you. You mentioned you were leaving town after Billy's service, so me and Diego agreed to let it go."

"Go on then. Tell me."

Gabriela said, "A few months ago, the cage league started up again. Only this time the games take place across the border in Agua Prieta."

"Don't tell me it's organized by Juan Carlos?"

"It is."

"Same rules?"

"Except there's more fighting than ever. Juan calls the new league the Elite Mix, but on the streets, people refer to it as the 'Death Mix.' If you ask me, I haven't seen much in the way of skill. I'm sure Diego would agree, but that league is mostly just a bunch of thugs. You know, fight first, shoot last. Some players have gotten seriously injured. A few have been taken to the emergency room. I heard someone eventually died from his injuries."

Shaking his head, Troy replied, "I knew he'd take it too far."

She fished a cell phone from her purse and started searching for a video on YouTube. "Must be a few thousand who show up for the games."

"Thousands? For real?"

She nodded. "Whoever they can jam into the warehouse."

"So, what are you saying, Miguel—"

"Miguel is the champ," Diego injected. "He's like 18-0. They call him Macho Muchacho now."

"Undefeated, huh?" But Troy had smoked his ass twice.

"Then again," Diego went on, "Miguel hadn't really played anyone. Not until a couple weeks ago when Billy showed up."

"What? You mean Billy went there?"

"We called you, but you didn't answer your phone."

All those messages on the answering machine, he recalled. All those warnings he had ignored with the push of a delete button.

"We tried stopping him," Diego said. "Honest. But he wouldn't listen."

Gabriela had found video of a match between Miguel aka "Macho Muchacho" and Billy, who had BILLY THE KID on his jersey. It was a one-on-one game from ten days ago. She pushed play and then handed Troy the phone. Someone had put together game highlights. A slash to the rim. A string of 3-pointers. Multiple fights breaking out.

"Billy the Kid was a freak," Diego spoke while Troy's eyes lit up. "You see it, right?"

It was true. Billy looked incredible. Troy had never seen his brother play with such intensity. He had even bulked up and had a new Greek warrior tattoo on his shoulder. "He looks … uncoverable."

"That's an understatement," Diego replied.

Billy slammed on Miguel, then flexed his arms and shouted at the crowd. Troy had no idea his brother could get so much lift. "Jesus. That really him?"

"He grew three inches while you were gone."

"Damn."

"And he was a step quicker than Miguel."

Billy did a crossover, got Miguel to stumble, and then stepped back and drilled a long 3-pointer.

Troy didn't know what to say. The story was unfolding before his eyes and he had a good sense of how it was going to end.

"Billy was in a zone," Diego went on. "I mean Miguel was fouling him hard, but he kept getting up and dropping his shots, swollen black eye, busted lip, and all. The game went back and forth. In the final minutes, Billy had the momentum. It was his game to win. Except, as you can guess, the big fix was in. Juan Carlos would not allow him a victory. In the final minute, Billy came up short on a ridiculous traveling call and then a game tying basket that was waved off."

Gabriela tucked away the phone. "Here's the thing," she said. "Billy was pissed off. Like I've never seen him pissed. He went home and posted a lot of shit on social media. He called out Juan and The Macho Boys, saying the Elite Mix was rigged."

Troy was stunned. Billy had wavered from the plan, instead of focusing on school like he had promised. "I didn't imagine any of this would happen," Troy said softly. "He wasn't stupid like me. He was always the responsible one."

Diego shook his head. "You know that. I know that. But Juan Carlos doesn't like to be disrespected. Did Juan kill him? I don't know. But three days later, Billy was dead."

Troy groaned. "Damnit."

"We told the cops everything."

"This is my fault."

"No," Diego insisted. "Billy knew what he was doing. He wanted to play. Me. You. Nobody could have stopped him from playing in the Mix."

Fight the Way Back

In the morning, Troy parked the truck by the Dollar Tree and hoofed it across the border.

He knew these streets. Back in the day, when his mother was sober and his dad alive, they'd had friends in Mexico. His father was buddies with many of the Mexican firemen. Sometimes, on Friday nights, their families met at restaurants in Agua Prieta to eat what his father insisted was "real Mexican food." But times had changed in the years since the tragedy in Afghanistan. More and more, life in Mexico was a twisted tale of economic hardship, drug trafficking, and political corruption.

He walked with his hands in his pockets. It was clear skies. Maybe 50 degrees. The sun on his skin was like a warm embrace. To hide his identity, he wore a long-sleeved Under Armor shirt, the Phoenix Suns beanie, and sunglasses. Passing a furniture store, he caught his reflection in the window; his facial hair was the length of NBA basketball star James Harden's beard.

Trying to blend in with the locals, as much as a tall, bearded gringo in shades could, he walked by a road crew ripping up asphalt with a jackhammer. The jarring sound jolted through his eardrums and kept him on edge. Inside, ever since he woke up that morning, his mind had been tearing into the list of suspects, Juan Carlos, Mistah Krunch, P-Brain. Any of them could be guilty. He was also thinking about the hundred grand on his head. *That was a lot of jack.* Moving down the sidewalk, he stayed on the lookout for potential assassins, his eyes darting here and there, searching the streets for sketchy souls; no doubt someone was willing to take him out.

On Avenida 4 he passed the Hotel Sonora Inn and made his way to a popular shopping district. By then, full paranoia had set in. Was someone following him? A killer standing across the street? A machete-wielding butcher hiding around the next corner? In the event of trouble, the Mexican police would likely turn the other way. The Federales were rooted in corruption. South of the border, fifty bucks and a firm handshake went a long way when cutting shady deals.

If only you had your gun, he thought.

Or another set of eyes.

It was a defining moment. Knowing he was a wanted man, with a bull's-eye on his forehead, and a target on his back, he had crossed the border in pursuit of justice. To say he was risking his life to find his brother's killer was only half-true. Thing was, he had also gone rogue for himself. For the Blake family's honor. Ignoring the advice of Sergeant Jones, and seeking retribution, was only the beginning.

He jaywalked with a group of Mexicans and passed a Permex gas station.

The Spanish style architecture, red-shingled roofs, and familiar beer advertisements painted on walls—Carta Blanca and Tecate—gave the town a distinctive Hispanic flair. Most of the buildings were unimpressive and looked to be in varying states of disrepair, with cracked adobe walls, patched stucco, and broken roof shingles.

He passed his mother's favorite restaurant and a leather shop where his dad had purchased his cowboy boots.

Now the memories flooded back.

Mom and dad.

Little brother.

Together, walking the streets in search of a bargain and spicy food.

A few blocks away, he finally encountered a poster promoting Juan's Elite Mix basketball league. There, along the wall of a taqueria, was the face of a pretty-boy Latino player pitted against a Mayan-looking dude:

GUAPO VS EL TUCAN
JANUARY 18
AT THE ELITE MIX

Troy used his cell phone to locate the Elite Mix club in a warehouse district six blocks away. Following the directions, he started down the sidewalk, passing several bars and a seedy hotel. At an alley, a mangy cat jumped in his path and then glancing over a shoulder he saw two guys exchanging cash for something in a paper bag.

All around him now, the Mexican border town came to life: the squeal of car brakes, kids selling Chiclets gum, stylishly dressed moms, and a bustling taco stand with its smell of cooked pork. Again, and again, he felt watched. He was sweating and his face was hot with stress. Every young man on the street was a potential assassin.

Fifteen minutes later, he arrived at the Elite Mix arena, a three-story brick warehouse in the heart of what friends called "El Crimeville." Here thieves, pimps, and drug dealers ruled the night. If you needed something from the underworld—a gun, a coyote, a hit—you found it on these dangerous streets. However, in broad daylight and with little more than rats for companionship, the boarded-up warehouse neighborhood felt more like a ghost town.

And yet the Elite Mix breathed life. The building had a fresh coat of paint and an entrance jazzed up by sparkling glass doors. He peeked through the tinted windows and viewed an entrance hall with space-age chairs, sports art, and basketball memorabilia.

Stepping back, he read a sign on the door and learned that DJ Taquito spun his records here. The Mix nightclub slash basketball arena was open on weekends, with one-on-one games played on Saturday nights.

Like standing outside a movie theater, a row of posters promoted past and upcoming hoops battles.

To his left, an artist had created a masterpiece with warrior flair. The poster was the most spectacular basketball art Troy had ever seen. His eyes fell in. It featured Miguel Ángel in his turquoise uniform with a rattlesnake around his neck and Billy with crossing bandoleers across a black jersey, a rifle in one hand and palming a ball with the other. The hype. The showmanship. The glory. He understood what drove his brother to join this league.

The poster read:

MACHO MUCHACHO VS BILLY THE KID
FOR THE CHAMPIONSHIP OF SONORA

Fueled by competitive hunger, and the desire to be champ again, Troy followed the row of posters along the brick wall, each print a memory of past games; reeking of legend, of something bigger and more exciting than the NBA, with headlines recognizing newcomers and rising stars.

SHOTIME VS DRAMATICO XXX

NUKE BALLER VS EL CAPITAN EXCELENTE

EL NANO VS THE WORD

He had never heard of these players. All of them were Latino or black. They looked like athletes, tall and long-limbed, with lean bodies and that certain "unstoppable" gleam in their eyes; but did they have the game to back it up? Or was it all for show?

A vacant lot next to the building caught his attention. A chain-link fence with green plastic slats walled off the area. Troy couldn't see over the fence but following the steel barricade around a corner and entering an alley, he found a section with missing slats. Now, peeking into the yard, he saw a basketball court with a chain net.

A few feet away, at a gate locked with a large padlock, he came across a flyer with a huge headline:

$500 PRIZE
FIRST TO BEAT MACHO MUCHACHO
OPEN CALL TO BALLERS
GET YOUR CHANCE
THIS SATURDAY NIGHT

Troy scoffed. Five hundred bucks? To beat Miguel?

"They say he's unbeatable," a young Mexican said. He had long hair and wore a Club Tijuana soccer shirt and headband. A stack of Elite Mix posters and a stapler filled his hands.

"What'd you say?" Troy jumped, startled.

"Macho Muchacho. Unbeatable."

"For real?"

"Si."

"You mean Miguel Ángel?" Pointing at the poster. Then with sarcasm, Troy added, "That guy?"

"Si. The great Muchacho is even better than LeBron James."

Troy snickered, and thought, *Lebron?* "I could beat Muchacho."

"Maybe in your dreams, amigo."

This, Troy knew, was a conversation going nowhere. The slim Mexican had no idea who he was. He probably thought Troy was some kind of deranged fan. "Okay," he said in surrender, "how does a guy get a shot at the so-called Macho Muchacho?"

151

"Do you play basketball, amigo?"

"You know it."

"But are you any good?"

"Like I said, I can beat Muchacho."

"Well, normally you'd have to work your way into the Mix League. Win a few games. Earn some respect—"

"I don't have that kind of time."

The Mexican shrugged. "In that case, if you want to play him—?"

"Oh, believe me I do."

"Then show up this Saturday." He pointed toward the basketball court on the other side of the fence. "There'll be a shoot around. If you're lucky the organizers will choose you to play Muchacho on Saturday. Then you will have a chance to win the money."

The cash prize meant nothing. He only wanted a shot at Miguel. Was it possible? *No.* Juan would never allow him to play his champion, because he knew who would win; besides if he spotted Troy's face, he would have his boys detain him, rough him up—or something worse.

His eyes on the court, Troy felt himself slipping back to the glory days, to the sparkling hardwood, to the bright lights, to the screaming fans. He turned to the Mexican, and said, "Did you really say, 'better than LeBron?'"

But the young man had already walked away.

How long he stood there dreaming about an epic game versus Miguel, dunking on him, rejecting his shots, draining threes, he didn't know. However, at some point in the daydream, he heard boots stomping on the pavement and saw thugs approaching from the other end of the alley.

Three pissed-off looking dudes.

One of them was Krunch.

Troy took a step, then started running in the opposite direction.

They were right on his heels. No matter how fast he ran. Right there. His pursuers were surprisingly quick. Regardless of the street he took, one of them was always an arm's reach away.

When they split up, Troy's mind went on the defensive: which direction would someone come from next?

He ditched the first guy by grabbing a broom from an old lady and whacking him across the face, then knocking the wind out of him with rapid blows to the stomach.

On the next street, another dude tried to pounce on him. Backpedaling, Troy ran into the road and slid across the hood of a moving Honda Accord, before landing on the pavement and slipping into a crowd of pedestrians. Behind him, he heard screeching brakes followed by a *thump*.

Without slowing, Troy worked his way toward the border crossing, located maybe three or four blocks away. He thought he was taking a shortcut when he descended into a narrow alley with a dumpster that smelled like garbage and rotten Mexican food.

Passing through, he entered a busy marketplace where street vendors sold blankets, novelties, and other trinkets.

And then suddenly Mistah Krunch was moving toward him. "Hey, you," he heard the gang member's voice. "Stop!"

Troy dodged between the stalls of food and household items, slid past a couple of people, but the muscle-bound guy gained speed and tackled him into a bin of fruit. Rolling in bananas and apples, Krunch missed with a headbutt, before pinning one of Troy's arms behind his back. He was about to lock him down when Troy poked him in the eye and broke free.

"Mother f—" Krunch shouted angrily, hands on his face, while Troy jumped up and escaped through an archway that lead to an indoor shopping bazaar.

Mariachi music played over speakers.

He found a small shop and pretended to be a customer, hiding behind a rack of men's shirts and a wall of luche libre wrestling masks.

It occurred to him now. They knew what he looked like. With a beard. Without a beard. And yet here he stood, in front of an assortment of masks.

Then an idea crossed his mind.

He picked up a silver mask with white lines around the eyeholes and mouth. Maybe, just maybe he could hide his identity and enter that Saturday night shoot around.

A shopkeeper with a pencil thin mustache approached.

"What do you think, amigo?" the Mexican asked. "You like?"

"Si," Troy stammered, reaching for his wallet. "More than you can imagine. I'll take it."

FLEEING MEXICO, he drove straight to Big Pig's Pizza in downtown Douglas. His mind was buzzing: Saturday was six days away. He needed to get in shape. Physically. Mentally. If Krunch could chase him down, and Diego could beat him one-on-one, then Miguel would be a fearsome match.

Instead of pizza, he ordered a salad with chicken.

And he drank water.

Lots of water.

Was there time to resurrect The Outlaw? Troy had never really played the part of underdog. Since second grade, he had always been the best player on the floor.

He watched the Arizona Southern basketball game on the television and finished his third helping of greens. Diego and Jackson were having a decent game, but the rest of the team sucked. After the game, he drove to the college.

He entered the gym, passed by the weight room and walked to Chavez's small office. The coach was sitting at his desk. He wore pleated dress pants, a red shirt, and tennis shoes. "I don't have time for the damn media," he spoke on the telephone, but abruptly ended the conversation when Troy waved from the doorway.

"Tough game," Troy said sympathetically. "You almost pulled it out."

"Hey, bud," Chavez replied, spinning in an office chair. The coach's love/hate relationship with the media was always entertaining—especially during a losing streak.

"Taking some heat from the *experts*?"

The coach nodded. "Damn local beat writers. And their stupid questions. What do they know about match-up zone defense?"

"To be honest, Coach, the team didn't look very good tonight."

Chavez frowned. "I know. I know. Some of the new guys just don't get the game plan."

"They'll come around."

"Let's hope so."

"We did, remember?" However, it was a sore subject. Last season, following the deadly incident with the baseball bat, Troy had left the team, his fate suddenly in the hands of the Cochise County judicial system, while Miguel fled to Mexico. The Scorpions lost the remainder of their games.

"By the way, I already mailed off that school paperwork."

"Thanks."

"And I called the university's Athletic Department and spoke to the basketball coach."

"Appreciate it."

"He's eager for you to walk on."

"Cool."

Truth was, Troy didn't really care Chavez was on the ball. Going to college, and playing basketball again was the furthest thing from his mind. Ever since Billy's ceremony, he hadn't really given much consideration to his future playing days.

"So, tell me," Chavez went on, "what's up?"

"Well, since the team has away games this week, I was

wondering if I can borrow a few balls."

"Borrow?"

"To shoot around."

Chavez twirled a pencil. "I'm happy to give you the keys to the gym. You would have the place to yourself."

"Thanks, coach. But if you don't mind, it means more to play on my family court."

"I understand." Chavez leaned forward. "But hey, it seems like something is on your mind. Want to talk?"

"No."

"Look, if you ever want to—"

"I'm okay, Coach. Really."

Chavez raised an eyebrow. "That police officer you spoke to the other day. Sergeant Jones."

"What about him?"

"He stopped by my office. Was asking about you."

"Did he tell you about the hundred grand?"

"He did."

Troy shook his head. "And do you think I'm scared?"

"No." A pause. "But you've been asking a lot of questions. And he's worried you plan to take the law into your own hands."

"Jones is high."

Chavez looked Troy in the eye. "Just don't do anything stupid, okay?"

Troy crossed his arms. "What about the balls?"

"Sure. Take 'em. Take whatever you like."

TUESDAY MORNING. After a brief hailstorm, Troy bolted across the white desert, sloshed through a creek, and slashed between the creosote bushes like a tailback in pursuit of the end zone. Some fifty yards away, a coyote kept pace.

The things flashing through his head: how physically fit would he be by Saturday? Would the luche libre mask hide his identity? What about his brother's killer? Was it Juan? Krunch? Another member of the Macho Boys? He had checked Miguel off the list of suspects. A friend—even a former friend—would never do such a horrible thing.

Ten minutes into the run his calves were cramping up and he felt winded. Fueled by a red-hot hunger for justice, he ignored the pain and descended into a gully and up the next hill, where he stopped to catch his breath.

The answer to the first question was obvious: he wasn't going to be in peak shape.

Drenched in icy sweat, he gazed across the shrubby desert and down the long highway toward the adobe church, its bell tower rising above the landscape. After a short break, he was ready to follow the road to his brother's grave, until an idea popped into his head and he turned around.

He would try again later. But next time he'd set the countdown clock on his watch for twenty minutes. The cemetery was his target. *Could he get there before the alarm sounded?* That was the goal. If he reached Billy's grave within that timeframe, he was sure he would be physically ready to ball. And, importantly, one-step closer to finding his brother's killer.

Walmart had everything he needed to secure the campsite.

Using fishing line, he strung together a series of empty coke cans between the creosote bushes to make a simple alarm system around the property's perimeter. Anything that tripped the wire would rattle the cans and give him advanced warning of an intruder. He placed the lines high enough so only a human would trigger the homemade alarm.

It was mostly paranoia, Troy realized. His deepest fears were eating away at his mind. Yet, that didn't stop him from setting up four wireless motion detectors around his tent, just in case someone made it past the first line of defense.

Would The Macho Boys come for him in Arizona? Probably not.

When the job was complete, he called the cafe in Dutch Harbor and tried to convince Alice to give him Emma's phone number. Annoyingly, the woman repeated her advice to "leave the girl alone" before hanging up the phone.

Next, he dialed the cannery and asked to speak with Emma's father. The man might have given Troy the number, but he was away on safari. The secretary, who was friendly with Troy, apologized and said "It's a private number. You know how her father is. I could get fired."

Troy didn't press the issue, but asked, "Do you happen to know if she's dating Peter?"

The woman was silent for a moment. "I think so. Then again, not sure. Why?"

"Oh, just wondering."

He hung up, deciding to let it go. *Let her go.* Seemed Alice was right. Emma was back with Peter. At this point, as he plotted his revenge, and accepted the fact that he might end up in a Mexican prison or dead after everything went down, it no longer seemed to matter.

WITH THE DUST came the fire: the orange and yellow inferno burning on the horizon. As the sun dipped behind the jagged mountains, its fury burned like a Middle Eastern war zone. These cool sunsets, he thought. His parents used to talk about how Arizona sunsets were the most spectacular in the world. Aside from Alaska, and family trips to California (Disneyland, SeaWorld, and a Dodgers game) he hadn't traveled much, but had to agree.

Later, when darkness fell, and millions of stars were sparkling in the sky, he connected his iPhone to the truck's stereo and cranked Metallica.

"Tonight," he whispered, reaching for the headlight switch. Tonight was a dress rehearsal for the major beat down he planned to put on Miguel. He clicked on the vehicle's high beams and the family's basketball court lit up.

Climbing from the truck, he loaded ten basketballs into a Walmart shopping cart and pushed it across the cracked concrete slab.

He stopped at the 3-point arc and reached for a basketball.

Dribbling twice, he squared his shoulders, and then jumped and released.

The ball clanked in and out.

He took a deep breath and grabbed another ball.

Missed again. This time the basketball hit the front of the iron.

Frustrated, he went 3 for 10, growing more upset after each errant shot. His timing was off. His release. Everything. Stinking like this, how could he possibly be ready by Saturday?

He followed up the last miss with an attempt to slam, but the ball slipped from his fingers and bounced off the back of the rim.

Pathetic.

DOUBTS CREPT IN. And doubt, according to Chavez, was a basketball player's greatest enemy.

The philosophical coach had drilled this ancient Chinese proverb into Troy's head during his freshman season, the words of wisdom painted in big red letters in the Scorpions locker room. "Never doubt yourself," Chavez had said. "Who you are. Or what you can be."

The words resonated in Troy's heart.

"Keep after it," he challenged himself, "You can find your touch. And beat Miguel. After all, everything seems impossible until it's done."

Lying on the sleeping bag, he heard a buzz and whipped out his phone. A text from Diego:

DUDE LET'S MEET AT THE GYM

He ignored the message. And soon a text followed from Jackson:

WHAT UP, HOMEY? WHEN WE GONNA PLAY?

He ignored that text, too. An hour later, he received a message from Gabriela:

HOW ARE YOU? WANT TO TALK?

Troy responded to Gabriela, hoping it might put an end to their paternal concerns, texting a lie:

EVERYTHING'S GREAT. JUST CHILLIN WITH MOM.

Next, he clicked the Pandora app on his iPhone and let the sounds of his favorite metal bands fill his head, Godsmack, Disturbed, Five Finger Death Punch. Overcome by high school memories, he recalled that time he, Billy, Diego, and Jackson snuck into a Linkin Park concert in Phoenix, and grinned.

Now he read his brother's unread text messages. He owed Billy the respect of knowing what had happened with the recruiting ... and his dreams. Scrolling with a thumb, he learned about his brother's visit to the University of Nevada; and saw a photo of him at the school's Lawlor Events Center; and an image of him wearing a Wolf Pack t-shirt; and another with Chavez at a basketball game.

Another text filled the screen: this one a photo of a cute brunette with the words MY NEW GIRLFRIEND.

The next message was strange: it was a blurry image. At first, he thought it was the girlfriend, but examining closer, wondered, *wait, was that ... Miguel?*

He pinched his fingers and zoomed in.

Could be.

Might be.

Had to be.

Troy noticed the text was date-stamped January 4, the day Billy died. He felt a knot in his stomach. Miguel? His childhood friend was last on the list of suspects. But—

He placed a hand on his forehead. Had Billy attempted to identify his killer? Did he send the pic just in time before he was beaten?

The police had never seen this image or read any of Billy's text messages because his cell phone was locked and no one knew the password. So what would the cops think of this blurred image of Miguel? Was it proof?

Troy sat up. Eyes startled. Only thing that mattered was what he believed. And he believed it *was* proof. *All the proof he needed.*

Miguel Ángel was the killer.

CRAZY ENERGY. Troy sprinted like a cougar across the desert, dribbling a basketball on the dirt, charging over a hill, into a ravine, and running along the desolate highway. Knowing the killer's identity provided extra motivation. It also sickened him. How could a former best friend do something like this?

He was fifteen minutes into the run and getting closer and closer to the cemetery down the road.

You're the punisher.

You're the wrecking ball.

No one can beat you.

When his watch beeped, he stopped and slammed the ball onto the highway's cracked asphalt. Came up short again, he thought in a frenzy. *Can't beat the clock, can you?*

A car whizzed by.

Followed by a drop of cold rain.

And the sun moving behind a cloud.

It was risky to run the same pattern every day, but Troy was growing less and less concerned that a Macho Boy would come after him in Arizona. Touching the loaded gun in the bellyband behind his back, his heavy eyes scanned the desert for hitmen.

Anyway, it didn't matter.

Troy was ready for anything.

For anyone.

He sucked in a breath of fresh air. Preparing for Saturday was the primary focus. He knew what he had to do: turn around, go home, and aim for the cemetery tomorrow.

He jogged back to the campsite.

Everything revolved around preparation. Fitness. Skill. Attitude. And looking the part was important, too. He needed shorts and a jersey with his name on the back. Speaking of which, what player name would he go by? He couldn't show up as The Outlaw on Saturday night. The Outlaw was a wanted man.

Grabbing the keys to the truck, he hopped in behind the wheel and headed for Al's Sporting Goods on Third Street.

The Chosen One? No, lame.

Revenge? Too cliché.

The Muchacho Stopper? Kind of funny, but too long.

Driving by the Walmart he recalled the conversation he'd had a few days before with the checker. "You're infamous," the guy had said. *Infamous*. By definition, it meant someone who is well known for a bad quality or deed. Troy grinned.

At the sporting goods store he bought a red basketball jersey and asked the manager to stitch the name Infamous across the back, along with the number one.

"And I need it by Friday," he added.

"Sorry, we're backed up," the older man replied. "It'll take two weeks to get that made."

"Please, sir. Two weeks doesn't work."

"It's the best I can do."

Troy whipped out a wad of cash. "I'll pay you four times the amount for the jersey. Whatever it takes. I just need it by Saturday."

The man nodded, and said, "This must mean a lot to you, eh?"

"It does. More than you can imagine."

"Okay. You seem like a good kid. I'll see what I can do."

"Appreciate it."

Troy also purchased a punching bag. And when he got home, he hung the bag from a tall Palo Verde tree near the basketball court.

BY THURSDAY his shots still weren't dropping. Frustrated, he threw a basketball into the desert and went for a drink from the garden hose. How could he possibly suck so bad?

There was a moment when the anger subsided, and he imagined Emma's beautiful face, and her sweet, sweet smile. And he wondered how she was doing at school. Hopefully awesome.

But did she ever think of him?

Walking back to the court, he felt bummed out that she was back with Peter Portman. Like a dagger to the heart, Emma had sacrificed Troy in a game of boy meets girl. *How messed up was that?*

He bounced a ball on the concrete.

She used you to make Peter jealous.

Not cool.

Not cool at all.

Later, he stood beneath the shade of the Palo Verde tree and pounded on the punching bag, his knuckles turning red.

Punch.

For Miguel.

Punch.

For his act of betrayal.

Punch.

For justice.

Punch.

For the man who killed his father.

Punch.

For the man who deserted his post.

Punch.

For anyone who stood against him. Now. And tomorrow.

TROY SET the timer on his watch and dashed off.

Everything was in sync: his pumping legs, his forward swinging arms. For the first time since he started training, his chest wasn't burning either. Today, he could possibly outrun a track star. At least in a dash across the desert with obstacles like prickly cactus, sharp rocks, and venomous rattlesnakes in his path.

He darted along the trail, dipped into the ravine, raced up the hill, and charged onto the desolate highway. Down the road, the adobe church rose above the desert shrub and Palo Verde trees like a raceway's checkered flag.

Troy pushed himself, the mental clock ticking in his head. Faster now, faster. He sprinted to the parking lot, ran up to the church, and saw the cemetery. As he passed through a wooden gate, the sweaty t-shirt felt like it was icing up on his back.

Boom!

Just like that.

You did it.

On the way to his brother's grave, with the sacred grounds closing in around him, the alarm finally sounded on his watch.

Looking into the gray sky, a storm cloud loomed over the

Sonoran Desert. He appeared to be the only person in the cold, forsaken graveyard. Steps later, distant thunder rolled and he felt a drop of rain on his hand, and sunk to his knees before his brother's headstone.

Someone had recently visited and left a bouquet of flowers.

He cleared his mind and sat in silence, feeling his brother's presence. When he was ready, he said, "Billy this shouldn't have happened. I'm sorry. I let you down. But I swear to you, if it's the last thing I do, I will avenge your death."

Slowly, slowly, Troy relived the brotherly memories: roughhousing with dad, playing video games, shooting hoops after school. Succumbing to the sadness, he closed his eyes and felt his body grow weak. When the floodgates opened, the rush of emotions he had suppressed for days on end swept over his face and he wept.

Soon he heard footsteps.

Gabriela kneeled beside him and placed a soft hand on his shoulder. "Troy," she said, tears on her cheeks. "I saw you running on the highway. And turned back."

She gave him a hug.

He was too choked up to speak. Instead, he held her hand and remained silent. Troy appreciated her friendship. But did he ever tell her that? No. Probably not. He sat there until his eyes dried up and then he stood with renewed vigor.

"I'm going away," he confessed.

"Away? Where to?"

"Can't tell you." He looked at her seriously. If she knew what he was up to, she would try talking him out of it. She would go to the police. "I have important business to take care of."

"Don't talk like that."

"Trust me. It's what I must do."

"But—?"

"You know... all these years... ever since junior high. I don't have a truer friend than you."

"But—?"

"Goodbye, Gabriela."

ON FRIDAY, he grabbed a pair of scissors and leaned into the truck's side view mirror.

The beard was coming off. Saying goodbye to the fisherman, and hello to the baller felt like a cleansing of sorts. In his mind, the moment marked the epic second coming of the former hoop sensation known as Troy Hanson Blake.

He cut.

Trimmed.

Then grabbed a razor to finish the job.

Barely two weeks had passed and already Dutch Harbor, the stinky cannery, and harsh life on the crab boat seemed like a lifetime ago. In retrospect, the captain's advice: "Be a better man," "Rise above," and, "Do the right thing," felt more like adult brainwashing and an effort by the judicial system to mold a good citizen. And those self-help books he had read about controlling his anger? Nothing but psychobabble, he now thought. Like Orwell's groupthink. Or Mao's Cultural Revolution. Their "good" advice was a form of indoctrination.

They didn't understand. The people who were supposedly wanting to help "a kid" just didn't grasp what deep, deep down drove Troy Blake to the brink. How could they? They were old. And he was young.

"Born to ball," Troy whispered, wiping a smear of shaving cream from his face. Without empathy he added, "And live to punish your opponents."

He missed the cage.

The action.

The bloodshed.

Now, clean-shaven and denting the punching bag with his bare knuckles, he again vowed to crush anyone who came between him and his brother's killer.

That night, the Ford truck's high beams lit up the family basketball court. He had also placed tiki torches around the campsite: one for his father, one for his brother, and another for the love of the game.

He connected his phone's Bluetooth to the vehicle's stereo and put rock music on shuffle. Wearing black shorts and a smelly Arizona Southern sweatshirt, he taped a photo of Billy to the basketball pole and then pushed the squeaky-wheeled shopping cart to the top of the arc.

Next, like a contestant at a 3-point shootout, Troy grabbed a ball and let it fly from his fingertips.

Dropped ... all net.

Then another ball.

A swish.

Ball after ball launched in rapid succession, with the accuracy of NBA shooting legends Steve Kerr, Reggie Miller, and Ray Allen.

He didn't miss a single shot.

Feeling it.

Just like old times—*he was in a zone.*

Troy followed the tenth made basket with some serious elevation, completing an acrobatic reverse slam, and hanging onto the rim.

He dropped to the court with his muscles flexed.

Then he picked up the basketball.

It wasn't that the Outlaw had come home. The Outlaw was dead. Long, long dead. Tonight, however, marked a new beginning. Tonight, Infamous had arrived.

And on Saturday, vengeance would be his ...

The **Infamous** One

The Glock was everything. Power. Strength. Key to his revenge. But he couldn't just walk across the border with the loaded handgun. That was too risky. If frisking didn't find the weapon, a metal detector would. Troy gave it some thought. A carrier. He needed a carrier. And then it hit him: "Someday," he remembered Peavey saying, "someday you might need a lift to Mexico." The old rocker's words were prophetic. And so tonight, the Metal Church bus, with its Christian icons and heavy metal music, was the answer.

At Walmart, wearing a Phoenix Suns hoodie, black sweatpants, and big headphones around his neck, he slung a gym bag over his shoulder and boarded the bus.

Peavey nodded, but didn't say anything.

Moving down the aisle, three Mexican men and a woman with a baby wrapped in a blanket gazed his way. They were thin and gaunt like zombies. *Hey, what are you looking at?* Creeped out, Troy found a place to sit at the back of the bus and then leaned over with duct tape and attached the gun beneath the seat. Safe there, he trusted. Since the bus crossed the border several times a day, he put his faith in security being lax.

... and kept his fingers crossed.

Feeling anxious, Troy leaned back against the cushion and gazed out the window.

Lost in his head.

Reflecting on life.

His mom.

His dad.

His little brother.

The bus's engine rumbled while Peavey drove to the Douglas Port of Entry complex and joined a line of vehicles heading south.

The minutes passed like hours.

Eventually, with *Cat Scratch Fever* by Ted Nugent blasting over the speakers, Troy held his breath while a female U.S. Customs agent boarded the bus and flashed an identification card at Peavey.

The rocker stopped playing air guitar and turned down the volume.

Next, the agent made a quick sweep of the seats, asking the handful of *zombies* for a look inside their bags. Then, with his heart racing, it was Troy's turn.

"What's inside the bag?" the agent asked. She was buff, Hispanic, maybe thirty-years old.

"Basketball gear," Troy replied, unzipping the bag. "Here. Have a peek."

He spread apart the fabric and showed the bottle of Gatorade, the package of beef jerky, his shorts, and Jordans.

"What's up in Mexico?" she asked.

"Meeting friends."

Looking at him closer, she added, "You look familiar. You from around here?"

"Yup."

"Okay," the agent said, "enjoy your visit to Mexico."

Troy exhaled. He had exactly one hour to get to the Elite Mix arena. And he had the gun.

The bus crossed the border and eventually stopped at a

crowded cantina with a brick patio and festive lights.

The door swung open.

Troy clutched the bag and hopped off.

Peavey, who wore a faded 1985 Judas Priest concert t-shirt and leather jacket, hadn't spoken a word to Troy the entire ride. He was grim, pensive. Now he said, "Big game tonight, eh?"

"Yes," Troy replied with surprise. "How'd you know?"

"I know everything that happens around here."

Troy accepted the former roadie's words as gospel. "Then you must know what's at stake?"

Peavey flashed a devil horn sign, and said, "Take it to him, brother."

Slipping the bag over his shoulder, Troy responded with a thumbs-up before walking toward the Elite Mix Arena.

The turnout was epic.

Every wannabe and their brother wanted a shot at Juan's money. A crowd of some two hundred plus basketball players wearing everything from NBA jerseys to soccer uniforms had gathered in the alley for the shoot-around and chance to play. The more competition the better, Troy thought eagerly, slipping the silver wrestling mask over his head and stepping in line.

Most of his rivals were Mexican, though a handful of black dudes and some white guys were among the hopefuls. The quick eye-test suggested only a few were legit athletes; most of the players waiting along the chain-link fence were out of shape or too gangly.

He put the headphones over his ears and turned up the Godsmack. Stretching his legs. Rising on his toes. Just trying to stay loose. While everyone appeared hungry for the big payout, Troy felt certain he was the only one who simply wanted a shot at Miguel. And, with guitars and drums thrashing in his head, the only player who planned to commit murder that night.

Soon the gate opened and the line started moving. Guys were turned away for obvious reasons, too short, too skinny, too fat. A few protested, claiming they were legit ballers, but security grunts pushed them away—roughing up a reject or two.

By the time Troy reached the gate, he realized Mistah Krunch and P-Brain called the shots.

"What's your name," Krunch asked in Spanish, black eye and all. He wore jeans and an Alabama Crimson Tide sweatshirt.

Troy gripped the gym bag's strap and replied, "They call me 'infamous.' The infamous one."

Recognizing Troy's Spanish sucked, Krunch switched to English, "Infamous? I ain't never heard of you."

"Maybe because I've never played in Agua Prieta."

"Yo, and what's up with the mask?"

Troy shrugged. "It's how I roll, dude."

P-Brain and another thug mucked it up.

"So what..." Krunch leaned into Troy. Did he see something? The eyes of The Outlaw? "You're an American?"

"Yup."

"Where you from?"

Troy considered the question, before saying, "Marble City, Arizona." A lie. The cowboy kid in the *Willy Wonka* movie was from Marble City.

"Never heard of it."

"Look it up."

Krunch seemed to respect Troy's confidence. "Do you play college ball?"

"No. But I was the best player on my high school team."

Krunch sneered. "Yeah, right. That's what they all say."

Troy spun the ball on his finger. "One hundred bucks says I can shoot ten for ten from the line."

"Okay," said Krunch. "I like your attitude." Eying him from head to toe, he stepped away from the open gate, and added, "Let's see what you got."

Dribbling the basketball between his legs, Troy noticed he was the only white player on the court. Thus far, fifteen guys were shooting around, stripped down to their shorts or sweats, and trying to impress.

A Mexican whistled and mocked Troy for wearing the luche libre mask. A couple other players laughed. Ignoring the idiots, he tossed up a shot that dropped all net.

When he spotted Jackson's white afro, his heartbeat accelerated and he thought *crap*; and then he steered clear of his friend. This wasn't good. Even though a mask concealed his identity, and the Suns hoodie covered the tattoos, Jackson might recognize his voice.

"That's it," he heard P-Brain shout. Glancing over his shoulder, he watched the stoner lock the gate. "Let's find a worthy challenger for Muchacho."

Twenty players had made the cut. Judging the competition, all the missed shots, and the weak dribbling, the poser moves, Troy believed he was the best baller on the court—even ahead of Jackson. But what were they looking for? Maybe they wanted a scrub? A bench player? An easy win?

"Keep shooting," Krunch shouted to the players. "My eyes are locked on you. If you suck, you're out. From what I've seen you all suck."

Troy finally recognized the brute. Mistah Krunch had played college ball a few years back. His real name was Zach Thompson. Dude was a small forward who blew out a knee his junior year and never recovered. He had NBA talent. Could've had a decent career. Big house. Fast cars. And plenty of babes. Sadly, these days, he was just a thug for-hire.

Troy dribbled and shot.

He was in a rhythm, drilling 'em left and right, though sometimes another player's ball knocked his ball out from the cylinder.

Meanwhile, the former college basketball big man was shoving guys off the court, telling them they were "the worst ever," to "go eat a tamale," and "stick to soccer."

Rejected players copped an attitude, but eventually left the yard; one guy wearing a Rasheed Wallace jersey threatened to return later to kick "Captain Krunch's" ass.

Troy threw down a monster dunk and then looked around for a little respect, but Krunch wasn't paying any attention.

After picking up the ball, Jackson approached, and said, "Yo, homey, nice dunk. Where you from?"

From? Troy gulped. Marble Falls. *You know, the town where that kid in Willy Wonka lives.* But keeping to himself he dribbled toward the key and did a layup.

Before long, Troy and his former college teammate were the last players standing.

Krunch approached Jackson and said, "You versus the dude in the mask. One-on-one. Best player moves on."

"No problem," Jackson replied, taking the basketball in for an uncontested jam.

The action went back and forth. A smooth step back jumper. A cross over and drive. A throw down hammer dunk. Troy didn't keep score in his head, so wasn't sure if he was winning. A year ago, when he was practicing every day, and in the best shape of his life, he would have crushed Jackson. The score would never have been in question.

Troy pumped a fist after drilling back-to-back NBA range treys. He had made his case, right? He had dunked. He had blocked. And he had stolen the ball multiple times. What more could he do?

On the next possession, having no intention whatsoever to shoot, Jackson lowered a shoulder and bulldozed right into him. Absorbing the blow, Troy threw up his hands and backed off with a smug grin.

I'm invincible.

Ten times the talent.

I'll smoke you.

They traded buckets until Jackson mauled him at the rim again.

Troy landed hard but was okay. Showing no emotion, he shrugged off the attack and retrieved the basketball.

"You're weak," Jackson spat, pushing him into the pole. "Me. Muchacho. Everyone will tear you up."

Troy's hands tightened into fists. If it came to it, even a step slower, and a little off his game, there was no question he could kick his friend's butt. Except he didn't want to go to blows with Jackson. Fighting a buddy right now wasn't cool. Instead, he took a deep breath and dribbled away.

But when he set for his next shot, Krunch suddenly appeared from nowhere and slapped the ball away. "You're out of here," he roared at Troy. "Adios."

"What?"

"Done."

"But he ain't better than me."

"See ya."

"Give me another chance," Troy pleaded, thugs in yellow shirts pushing him toward the gate. In a matter of seconds, they had escorted him out of the yard and secured the padlock.

In the alley, Troy ripped down the $500 TO BEAT MUCACHO poster and stood with his hands on his waist, irked by Krunch's wrong, bad, terrible, and stupid decision. *What was Troy going to do now?*

His head was already organizing the next steps. He could join the league and work his way up. Or he could enter the Elite Mix arena that night and confront Miguel before he stepped onto the basketball floor.

Something must be done.

He started for the street. When he reached the corner, he heard Krunch shout, "Yo, masked man. Come back. I changed my mind."

"I sent him packing," Krunch explained. "Didn't recognize the guy with his pimped-out white hair. But someone else did. He plays here. And we were clear that no Mix players could participate in tonight's game."

"So, I'm in?"

"Yes."

Hell, yeah. "Cool."

"Problem is," Krunch said, "Jackson worked you good."

"I was sticking to the fundamentals."

"Play like that against Muchacho, and he'll destroy you."

"You haven't seen the complete arsenal."

"Well, I hope you *got* medical insurance."

"Screw that."

"Just sayin."

"I can ball."

"I'll be the judge."

Troy heard guys rumbling on the other side of the fence. "The masked joker," someone yelled, "won't last more than five minutes with Muchacho."

Sore losers.

What did they know?

Krunch turned to his security people and ordered them to break up the crowd. After looking at his watch, he handed Troy a piece of paper, and said, "Rules. Read 'em." Before heading toward the building, he added, "Tonight, I expect to be picking pieces of you up off the floor."

Troy scoffed at the comment. "By the way," he said joyfully, "What happened to your eye?"

Krunch seemed put off. After a second, he said, "I kicked some annoying dude's ass. Any more questions?"

"No, I'm good." Troy smiled beneath the mask, then read the rules. They were basically the same—just as he had written them back in the day. Four ten-minute quarters. A twenty-second shot clock. No out-of-bounds. Clock only stops for timeouts, fights, and injuries. Best of all, fouls were almost nonexistent, which meant the game was sure to be a bloodfest.

Troy was prepared for anything.

He shot around and made most of his baskets. When a door swung open, he heard a basketball game, a crowd's massive roar, a ref's piercing whistle, and the heavy beat of rap music.

Growing impatient, he shot free throws.

Kept loose.

Stayed focused.

He could wait this thing out. Ten free throws or a hundred free throws. Whatever it took he was all in. He would sit through hell in order to come face to face with Miguel, the former friend who killed his brother.

Krunch returned an hour later, at 7:45 p.m. Dark now, stadium lights lit up the yard. "If you win," he said, "we pay cash."

Troy's shoulders tensed up. "I don't really care about the money."

"Don't care?"

Troy noticed a slim Mexican standing behind Krunch. He had long hair and wore a Club Tijuana soccer hoodie. Looking closer, it was the same guy who had told him to show up tonight. "What's the deal with him?"

"Meet Ignacio," Krunch said. "Your waterboy."

"What?"

"That's right."

"Yo, I don't need a waterboy."

"He'll set you up for the game."

"Okay, whatever," Troy replied, hoping they wouldn't inspect the gym bag and find the handgun. "Let's get this thing going. I'm freezing my balls off."

"Follow me," Ignacio said. "I'll take you to the locker room."

Troy gripped the bag and followed the Mexican into the warehouse. Along the way, he heard a dribbling basketball, squeaking shoes, and cheering fans. They were in a back corridor sealed off from the public. A fat security guard sat on a stool, keeping people clear of the area. Gazing over the man's shoulder and down a dark passageway, he saw a ramp covered in red carpet and bright lights shining down on the basketball court.

"The pre-game show," Ignacio said. "Players warming up the crowd."

"How long until my game starts?"

"About thirty minutes," Ignacio replied, leading him to a door with a sign: BAÑO DE HOMBRES. "You play after the current game finishes." Opening the door, he added, "Until then, this is your locker room."

"This? Seriously, dude?" The men's restroom smelled like piss.

"You should get dressed, amigo." Ignacio gave a polite nod and stood guard outside the door.

Men's restroom or makeshift locker room, the small space would have to do. Shrugging off the disrespect, Troy pulled the driver's license from his wallet and stuck it in the bellyband. Next, he placed the handgun at the bottom of a metal trashcan by the sink and made sure it was covered by used paper towels.

Safe there, he thought. *From thieves*. The loaded gun was a surprise for later—after he dominated Miguel on the court. If by some stroke of luck he made his way out of the arena in one piece (and he doubted he would), Troy needed the ID to return to the United States.

He tugged off the hoodie. Underneath he wore the red jersey with INFAMOUS across the back, black shorts with a stripe down the seams, and a black, tight fitting shirt to hide the tattoos on his arms.

178

He changed shoes, tying up his special edition "game only" black Jordans.

"Got to get this game started," he said, feeling the worst pre-game jitters ever.

He bounced the ball off the wall and imagined making moves.

At some point, he puked in the toilet.

An announcer broke the dulled sound of Mexican rap music, something about Muchacho versus Infamous. Then there was a knock on the door, followed by P-Brain and Ignacio entering the restroom.

"Any questions?" P-Brain asked.

"Nope."

"Good. Let's go."

A bass drum thumped. A flash of dizzying rap jabbed. Emerging from a short tunnel and standing at the edge of the red-carpet ramp, he watched blue laser lights shoot across the open warehouse, electrifying a crowd of what? Maybe several thousand fans?

Ignacio escorted him down the ramp, which split between the bleachers. The hoops arena was spectacular, a blend of Mixed Martial Arts craziness and post-apocalyptic doom. After his eyes adjusted to the flashing lights, he gawked at the thirty-foot high cage surrounding the hardwood.

His jaw dropped.

Elite Mix banners hung from the walls. Each displayed the names and accolades of star players. The most prominent banner showed Miguel's face and proclaimed him the undefeated champion.

By then boos and heckles flooded the music (that song, Snoop Dogg?) and a plastic cup filled with a margarita drink pelted Troy in the head.

Ignacio did his best to protect him from the rowdy crowd and flying debris. Fortunately, they didn't have far to walk. Before the song ended, he was standing on the main floor where P-Brain unlocked the gate leading into the cage.

Troy stepped in.

The cage's high fence rose from the sidelines, eliminating any chance for out of bounds and it shot straight to the rafters like towering castle walls.

In full beast mode, and with jeers showering down from the stands, he moved onto the court with his shoulders back and fists clenched. Ignore the hate, he thought. Embrace these fans. Before tonight is over, you can win their hearts.

He walked toward the free throw line. The hardwood had a Chupacabra mascot painted in the key, along with the words ELITE MIX. A series of orange lights embedded into the 3-point line flashed with the music. If he didn't despise Juan Carlos so much, he'd give the jackass a high-five for creating such a cool place.

A moment later, the gate clanked open and Juan strolled into the cage with the spotlight. The ex-con had cleaned up his image and was looking suave in an expensive white suite, black shirt, dark shades, and gold chains. Tonight, he was more Hollywood rap star than ruthless kingpin.

Troy took a heated step toward the guy. The gang leader had likely ordered the hit on Billy. Even so, reeling back his anger, he stopped before striking him. Juan's fist didn't kill your brother, he reminded himself. *Stay focused on the target.* You want Miguel. Later you can deal with the conspirators.

Heavy bass.

A guitar riff.

Strobing lights.

DJ Taquito spinning vinyl from a balcony.

Juan held his arms in a V and soaked up the cheers. The palms of his hands were begging for more and louder noise. When the music cut, he accepted a cordless microphone from P-Brain and welcomed the "basketball fans of Agua Prieta" to the main event, telling them drinks would be half price after Muchacho "kicks his opponent's ass." The crowd responded with a thunderous roar.

Juan approached Troy, and said privately, "I like it."

Troy wasn't sure what he meant. "Like what? Snoop Dogg?"

"No. The luche libre mask."

"Oh."

"It's good for the show."

"Glad you approve," Troy said with disdain.

"My people tell me you can ball."

"You know it."

Juan bathed in the mob-like excitement that rattled through the bleachers. "Look at them," he said excitedly. "They can taste the blood. Like lions ready to feast. Yet, I wonder: will you deliver tonight? Will you give them what they want?"

"Oh. I will. Believe me. I will."

"Excellente." Then pointing to the luminous backboard, Juan added, "See those sparkles? Hundreds of diamonds are embedded around the edges of the backboard. And the top is crowned with a Burmese ruby." A red gemstone about the size of a walnut gleamed near the top of the glass. "You are looking at the most expensive backboard in the entire world, gringo. Worth more than a million dollars."

Troy was unimpressed.

Suddenly the lights went out, and film score music kicked on. The song sounded like something from a spaghetti western movie, maybe *The Good, the Bad and the Ugly*.

On cue, Juan returned to the spotlight, his big charisma perfect in the role of Mix promoter, a golden smile stretching from ear to ear. "And now," he said in Spanish. "Ladies and gentlemen, let me introduce the challenger, from Marble Falls, Arizona, standing at six foot four, the masked baller, he who dares step into the cage... *and I fear for his life* ... the player known as Infamous."

A roar of boos showered down.

"Oh, this is ugly," Juan said to Troy. "They always hate

Muchacho's opponent. But nothing like this."

Troy got the message. Tonight, he would play the part of villain—or maybe red meat for the wolf. "Then let's give them what they want."

Juan grinned.

Next, the lights began to strobe, and smoke appeared by the red-carpet as Macho Muchacho entered with his posse to wild cheers and a Mexican rap version of Queen's *Another One Bites the Dust*.

"And now I give you," Juan spoke with a long drawl, flames shooting up from a fire machine, "standing at six foot three, the undefeated champion of the Elite Mix, with a perfect record of 18-0, from Agua Prieta, Mexico, the human highlight reel... the high-flying slammer... the lady lover... Macho Muchacho!"

Troy's hands were sweaty. He wasn't sure how he would react when he came face to face with his brother's killer. But one thing he knew: he would destroy Miguel at the rim, make a fool of him in front of his adoring fans, before putting the gun to his head.

Wearing a big smile, Miguel blew kisses to the crowd while girls pitched red roses his way. What, did Macho Muchacho think he was the Rose Parade queen or something? His former friend had bulked up and had new tattoos to go with his unrestrained confidence.

Five minutes passed before he finally entered the cage and got in Troy's face. Then they stood there. Both players embraced the spotlight like prizefighters in full showdown mode, refusing to blink.

"I'm gonna make you bleed," Miguel said between gritting teeth. "Hear me? Bleed."

"Dude," Troy replied, "I'm just trying to figure out who I'm supposed to play."

A vein snaked above Miguel's eyebrow.

It was difficult to remain cool. The longer they glared into each other's eyes, the shorter Troy's fuse shrunk. Just say something, Muchacho, he willed his enemy to defy him. One more thing. And you will meet my rock-hard fist. His heart racing, he was an impulse from snapping when a black and white stripped referee broke the tension by handing him a basketball. "House rules," the ref said, "challenger shoots a free throw. You make it, you bring it in."

"No problem," Troy replied, bumping shoulders with Miguel on his way to the free throw line.

After the crowd hushed, he dribbled twice and shot the ball, but hit the front of the rim.

Damn.

Nerves.

The fans roared in favor of Macho Muchacho and chanted, "Macho... Macho... Macho..."

START OF 1ST QUARTER

INFAMOUS   MUCHACHO

00   00

Dribbling in, Miguel lowered a shoulder and bulldozed into Troy, launching a forearm while slipping inside for a layup off the glass.

The crowd responded with a booming cheer.

That easy?

Troy shook off the blow, took the ball from the referee, and followed with a slashing layup of his own. "Hey Nacho Cheese," he shouted. "The Too Slow store called. They're running out of you."

"Keep taking, Red Robin," Miguel bit back, mocking Troy's hidden identity by comparing him to Batman's sidekick.

Troy planted his Jordans in the paint. No more easy layups, he was thinking. Challenge everything. Stick to him like glue.

Muchacho's hard-hitting style of play caught him off guard. Not only had his former friend gained 25 pounds, but he was a force in the post and had mastered the art of pushing off. Again, and again, Miguel took the basketball in for an explosive layup and a power jam, rolling over Troy like a Desert Storm tank as he struggled to hold his position.

Up by two, then four, and then seven, Miguel was all smiles when he called a timeout and strutted to his timeout zone at the back of the cage.

Troy walked to his area, indicated by a black circle on the floor. The scoreboard and lights along the three-point arc were flashing to an energetic rap beat.

1ST QUARTER

INFAMOUS	MUCHACHO
6	13

Sweat dripping, Troy stretched the leather mask away from his chin and breathed; more than anything, he wanted to yank the damn thing off.

"You're doing good," Ignacio said, slipping Troy a bottle of water through a small hatch in the fence. "Most players would be down by ten or more."

Troy nodded, heaving a breath.

Only the referee and competing players were allowed inside the cage, though two thuggish guys in yellow jerseys (the "Bounce Crew" written across their shoulders) lingered near the gate, ready to burst in and break up a fight.

Troy was frustrated. He needed to play more aggressively. Working out a cramp in his calf, he overheard Krunch shout something to Muchacho about abandoning his jump shot. "This game might be a cakewalk for you," the thug shouted at Miguel.

"But don't get lazy, ya hear?"

After the referee blew the whistle, Troy returned the bottle to Ignacio and tied up his kicks.

A cakewalk?

With 4:07 on the clock, Troy slammed his former friend into the fence, stole the ball, and nailed a mid-range jump shot.

The crowd let out a collective gasp.

A few cheered for Infamous. "How's that for cake?" he said.

Miguel shoved Troy. "Don't worry, you still get your participation trophy."

But Troy pushed back.

After a quick exchange of blows, and a bomb landing on Troy's cheek, he lunged forward and pulled Miguel into a strangling headlock, pounding a fist into his face two, three times before the Bounce Crew stormed the cage and broke up the brawl.

The referee warned the players about fighting. "I will call a technical on the next player who starts a fight," he said. "This isn't luche libre. It's basketball."

Troy huffed. Nodding his head, and feeling a little battered, he backed away from his brother's killer. Stay cool, he reminded himself. Don't let him win the psychological battle.

The referee blew the whistle and the game clock started.

On the next two possessions, Troy turned the ball over and mishandled a rebound.

He was rusty. The cage molded players in ways that regular basketball never could. During his time away, in the canary, on the crab boat, Troy had lost his combative edge.

Miguel thundered back, dipping a shoulder and knocking him away, before pulling up for a short jumper. After the ball dropped through the net, he thumped Troy on the chest, and said, "Now that's how you do it!"

Speed versus muscle.

Something had to give.

Miguel's defensive mindset for the remainder of the quarter was to hack Troy every time he attempted a shot. Because he was a step quicker, and a little more agile, Troy was often able to slip away and shoot before Miguel's hand (and sometimes a fist) came crashing down.

At the buzzer, Troy was trailing 12 - 20.

And he was amped up.

He wanted to punch something.

Anything.

Heck yeah, Troy thought excitedly, pumping a strong fist and smirking at the riled-up fans. He fed off their venom. *I'm in this. You didn't believe in me. But I'm in this!* He had missed a few shots, turned the ball over, and given up some easy buckets, but felt confident in his ability to adjust.

The referee pointed toward the gate and instructed both players to leave the cage for a ten-minute timeout.

"Stay close," Ignacio said, leading the way up the red-carpet. "It looks like you don't have many fans in Mexico."

Troy ducked for debris, but a bottle hit him in the shoulder blade, followed by a cup of beer.

Before leaving the walkway where the fat security guard sat on a stool stuffing a burrito into his mouth, he spun and saw Miguel and Juan mucking it up.

Yeah, Miguel, maybe you owned me, he thought bitterly, the beer suds dripping down his neck. *Owned me for the first quarter, anyway.*

Returning to the makeshift locker room, he asked Ignacio to wait outside.

Right away, Troy noticed the gym bag was missing. "What the—?" Then again, he had a feeling someone might steal it. That's why he had stuck the gun in the metal trashcan by the sink.

He removed the wrestling mask and examined his face in the mirror. The cuts and bruises didn't look too bad. Miguel's bloodied-up mug was far worse. He cupped his hand beneath the faucet and inhaled a swig of water.

Hydrated, he reached down and made sure the loaded gun was safe at the bottom of the trashcan, locating it beneath the layers of used paper towels. He was half-tempted to take the weapon to the basketball court and put it to Miguel and demand answers. Fast track the revenge. But now more than ever he wanted to beat his ex-friend. Stomp his sorry ass into the hardwood. Humiliate him. Down by eight, he believed the game was his to lose.

A minute later Ignacio opened the door and said, "time to go back to the court."

Keeping his face hidden, Troy slipped on the mask and headed for the door.

START OF 2ND QUARTER

INFAMOUS	MUCHACHO
12	20

Troy stutter-stepped, before sticking a deep three-pointer.

He felt a surge of confidence.

On the next play, he picked Miguel's pocket, rolled left and drove inside for a sweet layup but was pummeled after the shot.

He fell hard and banged his head on the hardwood.

The crowd roared.

Down on his back, he started to get up when Miguel stepped through his legs. With a taunting grin, his ex-friend pointed a finger, and said, "Hit the shower, Robin. Your game stinks."

"Say what?"

"You heard me."

The heat of battle was too much. Troy jumped to his feet and thumped Miguel in the chest.

"No fights," the referee warned, blowing the whistle. "We have a game to play, muchachos."

Miguel pretended everything was cool but then smirked and said, "Your skills are impossible to underestimate."

Seriously, dude? It wasn't exactly a bigtime dig, but Troy was revved up. This was the gang member who had beat his brother to death. As his Miguel swaggered toward the top of the key, he shot like a dart and tackled him to the hardwood.

Fists propelled like rockets but neither player landed a solid blow. The crowd loved it, thundering with excitement. Yet, it was mostly wrestling until the Bounce Crew broke things up.

Troy heard a whistle and watched the referee call a technical on him.

Miguel made his free throw.

A thirty-second timeout followed while a janitor cleaned up a streak of blood and a slippery spot on the floor.

"Don't let him bother you, amigo," Ignacio said, passing a bottle of water through the hatch. "You're in this game."

"It's all good." *But was it?*

The back of Troy's head stung. It felt pretty sore. Having a drink, he watched Miguel stop his bleeding nose with a tissue. Next, he looked across the court. On an elevated platform between the bleachers, Juan relaxed on a sofa with a cocktail in his hand. Two smoking hot women in tight leather pants sat on either side of him. Sexy stage props, he thought. They stroked the guy's ego. Made him look powerful. It reminded Troy of a smug Roman Caesar sitting on his throne and watching a gladiator battle. Beating Miguel and embarrassing the kingpin in front of the girls and the throngs of fans packed inside the warehouse would make the taste of revenge even sweeter.

He walked to the hoop and stood with his hands on his waist. Looking up, he noticed a small crack on the diamond-studded backboard.

When the ref blew the whistle, he accepted the ball and spun to face his opponent.

After rejecting a shot and picking the ball on repeat trips, Troy clawed his way back into the game and eventually took the lead after hitting a long three-pointer.

He was feeling it.

In a zone.

With hot hands, and some raw, in-your-face defense, Troy had sucked the energy straight from the crowd. Now he heard rumbling in the bleachers. *Who is this infamous player?*

After he went up by nine, bogus calls by the referee clouded the final minutes of the second quarter.

A travel violation.

A technical for a late push.

A string of hand-checking calls.

Arguing with the ref didn't help. It only resulted in another technical, which sent Miguel to the line for a free throw and the ball.

Pissed, Troy played through the bad calls. But the referee was a distraction, like a second opponent on the floor, and messed with his rhythm. Feeling the pressure, he missed a short jumper at the buzzer and shouted "fuck."

On his way to the locker room with a one-point lead, he glanced up at the backboard again: the crack was an inch longer.

Ignacio placed his hands on Troy's shoulders and ushered him toward the red-carpet. A thunderous boo shook the building. A death threat rang out, "Watch your back, Americano!"

"Ignore them, amigo," Ignacio said, heading up the ramp. "They are drunk."

Troy was irritated. The basketball game shouldn't be this close. The crooked referee was working against him. Déjà vu was the thing, right? *Exactly how they took Billy down.* It had taken restraint, everything he had, not to jack the ref up.

He stormed into the restroom and drank water without removing the mask. These long timeouts disrupted the flow. He just wanted to stay in the cage and ball. With his hand cupped beneath the faucet, Juan suddenly crashed through the door, followed by Krunch and some bald muscle-bound thug named "El Gorilla," a member of the Bounce Crew.

A weird feeling stung Troy's skin. Fuck, what did they want?

"Gringo, gringo, gringo," Juan muttered with a sneer. Toking on a joint, he approached Troy and slapped him on the mask. "I'm impressed."

"Yeah?"

"You are good. Really, really good."

"No big thanks to your blind-ass ref." Troy was suspicious of the locker room visit.

"Best of all you have that certain style," Juan plugged on. "I must admit, at first I thought the mask was a bit over-the-top. Part of me believed you were making fun of Mexicans. And my culture." He inhaled and blew smoke. "But now I understand. You are flamboyant. Like me, you peddle in the drama zone."

"Uh, if you say so."

"You could be a star in the Elite Mix."

Troy shrugged. He had his scope on Juan, too. The kingpin was a marked man. After Miguel, his day of reckoning would come. "So what's up?" he asked sharply. "You here for my autograph or what?"

Juan looked him dead in the eye. "For your information, I am a successful businessman, gringo. Week after week, I put on a show for these people. Most of them are young and poor. They live miserable lives. Many can't find a decent job. It's true, there's little hope for the future in this stinking town. So these fans come to the Mix games to party and lose themselves in fantasy. And," he added sharply, "the great Macho Muchacho is their hero."

Clearly, Juan hadn't expected a competitive game tonight. But now—like it or not—they had a nail-biter on their hands.

"Well, hang onto your freakin' seat," Troy said matter-of-factly. "Tonight's game might come down to the last possession."

"Possibly." Juan smiled nervously. "And yet I have a business proposition for you. A most respectable one."

"Oh?"

"Tonight was only meant to be an exhibition game. Not a real one-on-one competition."

"What's that supposed to mean?"

"It means I'd like you to step on the brakes, amigo."

"What?"

"You heard me."

"Step on the brakes?" Troy grabbed a towel and wiped the sweat from the back of his neck. "Yo, I came here to win."

"And I'm prepared to slip you two thousand dollars to lose."

"To what . . . throw the game?"

"Si."

"So, you're bribing me?"

"Depends. Do you need the money?"

"No, actually. I don't."

Troy didn't blink. He wasn't for sale. He was one hundred percent in—and determined to win.

Juan snickered. Then, giving Troy a mocking slap across the face, he whispered, "The hero must not fall."

"And I'm not throwing the game—"

Without warning, Juan slugged Troy in the stomach, knocking the wind out of him and buckling his knees. Again, he said, "The hero *must not* fall!"

As Troy attempted to catch his breath, Krunch pushed him to

the floor. "Don't be a fool, dude," the thug said, showering him with a handful of twenty-dollar bills before leaving the room with his boss.

When they were alone, Troy got on a knee and accepted Ignacio's hand for help. The Mexican waterboy asked, "You okay, amigo?"

"Yeah, I'm fine."

"I mean no disrespect. But these guys are serious. I would take the money and run. There is no shame in losing."

"Not a chance," Troy replied, peeling off the mask and wiping the blood from his lip. "Not a chance in fucking hell."

Recognizing Troy's face, Ignacio's eyes grew wide. "Hey... hey you're the American I met the other day."

Troy nodded. "Yeah, so?"

"So it's you!"

"Like I said . . . I can beat Muchacho."

With astonishment, Ignacio replied, "Who are you?"

START OF 3RD QUARTER

INFAMOUS	MUCHACHO
31	30

Who was he?

Troy was a player capable of stretching the lead. That's who he was. He came out on fire, drilling a 3-pointer, smashing a two-hand jam, followed by a killer crossover that tripped up Miguel. He talked trash with the referee and got slapped with another technical, which brought the crowd to its feet. "Two on one," Troy said, walking from the ref with his shoulders back. "Whatever. I'm good. Even you can't stop me."

In his head, he heard Coach Chavez riding him hard, "you're too slow," and, "you're leaving too much room." So, he stepped up his game, and attacked the rim, and played in-your-face defense. He was cleaning the glass, too. Preventing second chances. Checking easy buckets. The explosive, balls-out effort paid off. Halfway through the third quarter, and after a series of bogus violations called against him, the crowd turned on the referee.

"Stop interfering," a heavy Mexican shouted. "Let 'em play basketball!"

When Troy was penalized with another charge, he threw up his hands in disgust to encourage the boo birds.

And he got more than he asked for.

Fans booed, but they also tossed cups and bottles at the cage. Most of the debris clanked off the fence, the liquids pouring onto the floor and forcing a long timeout while a janitor mopped up.

The referee grabbed the microphone and called for order. "Por favor," he pleaded. "No more disruptions."

A handful of rowdy fans cheering for Infamous in the front row were quickly hauled away from the stands and led out the building.

Six minutes and twenty seconds later, Troy put Miguel on skates and nailed a fadeaway to take an eleven-point lead. Supercharged, he pointed a finger at Juan, and shouted, "Hit the brakes? Who, me? I'm about to shift into fourth gear, dude."

On the next play, Miguel slipped away and slashed into the lane for a layup; but Troy caught up and blocked the shot from behind.

In frustration, and no doubt feeling embarrassed, Miguel came after him like Mike Tyson, launching a fist that was followed by a wild uppercut.

Troy back peddled, quick on his feet, and made room for the guys in yellow to storm the cage.

Crazy.

He seemed to be orchestrating everything, from the game's fast tempo, to the frenzy in the bleachers, to the fistfights. Having fallen behind, Miguel's swagger was gone, his shoulders were hunched, and his eyes had that deer in the headlights glaze. Down 43 to 32, he was forced to play basketball instead of playing to the crowd. And he no longer spat out insults or called Troy "Red Robin" in mock of the masked sidekick.

Troy locked it down on defense and increased his lead.

A steal.

A slam.

A rushed shot.

A bomb.

With ten seconds left in the third quarter, Miguel drilled a three but landed awkwardly on Troy's foot and twisted an ankle. "Fuck," he shouted in pain, rolling on the floor. "Timeout. Timeout!"

Troy glanced at the backboard: the jagged crack was spreading like a subduction zone.

Wondering if the glass would shatter, he walked to his backcourt zone. Around him, Mexican rap and a dazzling light show entertained the crowd. In some ways, game stoppages were nothing more than a buzz kill. He wanted to keep playing. Before the timeout ended, he looked at Juan Carlos sitting on his VIP platform. The nervous kingpin had removed his coat and was rubbing a fist into the palm of his hand.

Yo, mess with my family, Troy was thinking. And this is what you get.

Miguel.

Juan.

Krunch.

Whoever.

All of you are going down tonight.

"Your ball," the referee shouted, thrusting the basketball into Troy's chest.

Troy groaned. Time for the exclamation point, he was thinking as Miguel limped into a defensive stance.

Glancing at Juan, Troy made a slit throat gesture with his finger, before dazzling the crowd with a speedy reverse layup and extending the lead.

"You sure?" Ignacio asked the moment they stepped into the men's restroom. "About playing to win?"

"It's the only way I play."

"But Juan is a powerful man. He is expecting you to lose—"

"Screw him."

"And the referee—"

"Even he can't stop me."

"Amigo, for your own safety, please take my advice and miss some shots. And whatever you do, stop provoking Juan Carlos."

"Not a chance."

Ignacio put a hand on his forehead, the stress showing in his strained eyes. "I'm sorry. I just work here. I'm a simple employee. I can't keep them from hurting you."

"No worries," Troy said, patting Ignacio on the shoulder. "But do me a favor, okay?"

"Si. Anything."

"Ask the DJ to play a song called *Thunderstruck* by AC/DC to celebrate my victory."

"A song?"

"Not any song. My theme song."

"*Thunderstruck*," Ignacio repeated. "Never heard of it."

"Trust me. The DJ knows."

"Okay, amigo. This I will do for you." He frowned. "However, I hope you lose."

Just then the door burst open. Juan, Krunch, and El Gorilla stormed into the restroom like robbers heisting a bank. "You're fired," Juan barked at Ignacio. "Leave now, and don't return."

As El Gorilla steamrolled, Troy put up his fists and punched back;

195

however, the big guy was too much to handle. Krunch swarmed, too. In Blitzkrieg fashion, the thugs managed to quickly put Troy in a strong chokehold.

"Let's see what the jerk looks like," Krunch said, starting to remove the mask.

"No," Juan injected, punching a fist into the palm of his hand. "Leave it on. The mask will hide the bruises. Plus, I don't want blood on my expensive Armani suite."

Troy struggled but couldn't free himself.

"We're done talking," Krunch sneered. "Time to pay the piper, sucker."

Minutes later, Troy was in a daze, lying face down on the tiled floor. How many times had they hit him? In the face. In the stomach. In the chest. It felt like he had a cracked rib or two, and blood was trickling from his mouth and out from the mask.

But it's not over, Troy thought with a jolt of pain. *Suck it up.* You have a quarter of a basketball to play. They stopped Billy with a fixed game. *Don't let them stop you!*

Inch by inch he crawled toward the trashcan, the cracked ribs making it painful to breathe, let alone move. Yet slowly, slowly he reached and pulled down the can.

Win or lose, you came to the Mix with one goal.

He grabbed the Glock handgun and with every effort slipped it into the bellyband behind his untucked jersey. Getting on a knee, the white undershirt sleeves smeared with blood, he stood and stumbled toward the exit, barely able to pull open the door.

From the arena, he heard the announcer declare the game "Over," forfeited because Infamous had refused to play due to a "game-ending injury."

Forfeit?

No way.

His eye swollen, he staggered toward the red-carpet ramp. Re-entering the arena, he heard a stranger's voice shout, "Look, it's

Infamous."

And someone else said, "He's back."

The spotlight came down and the Mexican rap music stopped.

After a few steps he surrendered to the pain and fell to his knees. *Get up.* His face tightened. *You can do this.* Crawling, he found the strength to stand and then stagger down the ramp.

"Don't quit," someone said in Spanish.

Row after row people encouraged Troy to keep moving. Now he flashed to life on the fishing boat, the sleepless days, pulling pots, his veins nearly frozen with ice. And he thought, that sucked, too. But you made it through the hardships. *Even with Radanovich riding your ass, you made it through.* With their shouts and cheers, he gradually reached the cage and stepped onto the court.

On the hardwood, Juan wore sunglasses and held a microphone. "Amigos," he said impatiently to the restless crowd. "The game has already been called in favor of the great Muchacho."

The booing fans roared back. "Let him play," a girl shouted.

"Yeah, let him play," said another.

Troy felt a sharp pang in his ribs and dropped to a knee. Never surrender, he thought with a fist. What they did to you. *To Billy.* He was slow to get up, encouraged by a faint chant that broke through the boos, "In-fa-mous ... In-fa-mous ... In-fa-mous."

"You are a fool," Juan said, Miguel standing behind him.

"No mas," the referee insisted. "The game is over."

"No," Troy insisted with clenched teeth. "I can play."

"Game over," the referee said again.

Juan looked at the rowdy crowd, a small but growing revolt on his hands. It seemed his reputation was on the line. Groaning, he finally said, "Okay. Let's finish this."

INFAMOUS   MUCHACHO

57   38

Each dribble. Every shot. It felt like someone jabbing a hunting knife into his cracked ribs. Worse, like the knife was twisting, turning, and shredding up muscle tissue.

Troy did his best to withstand the torture. Taking shallow breaths helped. But how was he going to survive the final ten minutes? He had to move. Had to run. Had to jump. His philosophy was to always play 100%, go full speed on each possession, run coast-to-coast like you're down by ten. He wasn't big on slowing the tempo, but given his injuries, Troy recognized with a 19-point lead, milking the clock might be his best option.

Fortunately, Miguel wasn't one hundred percent healthy, either. Slowed by a bum ankle, he was limping off the dribble and unable to get any major lift or take a quick step to the hoop. It didn't exactly level the playing field. The guy still had the physical advantage over Troy. As the minutes ticked away, and Infamous went scoreless, Macho Muchacho's comeback gained momentum.

A layup.

A jump shot.

Another layup.

A long two-pointer.

A fadeaway.

Troy did his best to hang on, tugging Miguel's jersey when he got away, throwing up a hand at the last moment to disrupt a shot. But his defense was pathetic. His offense even worse.

In agony, having watched Miguel score ten unanswered points, he used a timeout.

By then, five minutes and twenty seconds remained on the

game clock.

An eternity for Miguel's comeback.

And there was Juan, kicked back on the sofa with a cigarette and a cocktail. The expression on his said it all: *the hero must not fall.*

Troy staggered across the free throw line, a hand pressed against his ribcage. Just walk it off. Breathe in. Get some air.

The scoreboard read:

INFAMOUS   MUCHACHO
57   48

A stranger poked a water bottle through the cage. And a familiar voice said, "Dude, I can't believe you're here!"

It was Diego. And Gabriella was standing behind him. She looked terrified. *What were they doing at the Mix?*

"How'd you know?"

"Gabby's uncle told us."

"Uncle?" Troy had never met Gabriela's uncle. She rarely spoke about the guy. Apparently, he was a failed musician and deadbeat living in London.

"We got here as fast as we could. But dang this game is messed up. There's blood dripping down your neck. What happened?"

"I'll tell you later." With the lead slipping away, the presence of friends boosted his morale. "Anyway, I found proof," Troy said urgently, getting to the real heart of the matter. "Proof Miguel killed Billy."

"Miguel? For real?"

"He was there the day Billy died."

"But—"

"No matter what happens tonight. Win. Lose. He's going down."

"What's that supposed to mean?"

Troy made his hand into the shape of a gun and put it to his head. "It means the Latin lover is going down. Kiss kiss, bang bang."

"Hey," Diego shot back as Troy walked away. "Don't say that. Wait a minute!"

Troy's untucked jersey hid the Glock. Like a comforting hand, the weapon pressed against his lower back, just waiting for the right moment. "Stick around, brother," he said with a hidden grin. "Promise you. It's gonna be an explosive finish."

A mere ghost of himself, he exchanged baskets with Muchacho, shots simply thrown up and somehow rolling in. Miguel was exhausted and hobbling across the key, but like a fierce warrior, pulled it together and laid his body on the line. Just when Troy believed he might have enough resilience to milk the game clock and win by a point or two, Miguel crashed into him.

Troy toppled backwards and landed on his butt. *That one really hurt.* Gasping for air, he pushed himself to a knee. When he tried to stand, Miguel shoved him in the shoulder and laid him out flat.

The referee let the cheap shot slide and called for an injury timeout while Troy saw stars and struggled to his feet.

"You want to quit?" the referee asked. "And forfeit the game?"

With the girls draped around him, Juan kicked back on the sofa and unleashed a triumphant grin.

"No quit," Troy finally said, ears ringing. "I'm okay."

Another minute passed before the ref blew his whistle and the clock started.

"You're one tough hombre," Miguel admitted, dribbling the ball. "But you should've stayed down. Now I'm done toying with you." He spun away and performed a reverse layup and then struck a weightlifter pose.

The crowd, however, didn't respond with a favorable roar.

Troy thought he heard "boos."

At 63-62, with Troy holding onto an impossible lead, most of the fans had shifted their support; having cheered when Muchacho missed a shot, protested each time Miguel knocked him to the floor, and applauded as Infamous struggled to play on.

Somehow, even with a swollen eye, Troy had something in reserve to claw back on defense.

With under a minute, Miguel banged shoulders and stole the ball, worked some clock, and found the hops for one last power slam. The bucket gave him the lead with fifteen seconds left in the game.

"Timeout," Troy shouted, his ears ringing with a momentary deafness. He stayed in the key, taking slow breaths while Krunch and Miguel worked up their strategy for a last defensive stop.

The scoreboard read:

INFAMOUS   MUCHACHO

63   64

A nail-biter. Exactly like he had predicted.

The referee pointed a finger at Troy. Between the zany crowd, the beat of rap music, and his effed-up ears, he couldn't understand what the Mexican ref was saying. "Dude?" he shouted at the guy, his palms turned up, "what's your problem?"

Now he read the man's lips. "Your ball."

Oh.

Right.

Disoriented, Troy dribbled to a blue line beyond the 3-point arc where players officially started each possession.

This was it.

Game on the line.

The ref signaled for action and the clock ticked down: fifteen ... fourteen ... thirteen seconds ...

You got to stay smooth under pressure, Troy was thinking. He held the basketball against his hip and surveyed the lane. Left, Miguel's weakness? Or right, the element of surprise?

Miguel was quickly on him, feet in position and slashing his hands.

Troy dribbled.

He knew a hard foul was coming.

Lowering a shoulder and digging an elbow into Muchacho's chest, he created room and drove right toward the basket.

Four seconds …

The leap.

Three seconds …

His feet twisted into a pretzel, and with zero hope for blocking the shot, Miguel reached for Troy's upper body and wrapped him up like defending fourth and goal.

But Troy was the stronger bulldog. Fighting through the takedown, he wouldn't be denied the bucket. He had too much hops. Too much muscle. Too much determination.

With both hands on the rock, he carried Miguel on his back, reached for the hoop and pushed the basketball through the cylinder. At the same time, the rim snapped with the sound of a crack and an explosion of backboard glass.

Miguel hit the hardwood and landed on his back just as the clock expired.

A split-second later, Troy crashed on top of him, the gleaming shards showering down in a sudden hailstorm.

Everything passed in slow motion. The glass scattering across the floor. The fans rising to cheer. The referee, in a final act of desperation waving off the shot.

Before pushing himself up, Troy noticed the basketball bouncing away and the precious ruby sliding to a stop near his hand.

Deliberately placing a foot on his former friend's back, Troy climbed off the bloodied-up guy and faced the thunderous crowd.

Feel it.

Sweet victory.

With a sudden whoosh in his eardrums, he now heard their roar.

"Too late," the referee shouted in Spanish, waving hysterically at the scorekeeper. "Clock expired. Game over. Muchacho wins."

The crowd pushed back. They knew the truth. Troy had beat the buzzer.

It didn't matter. Troy had moved on. *Stay focused on the real reason you tied up your Jordans.* You have questions, he reminded himself. Serious questions.

Blood oozed from a broken nose and ripped flesh on his kneecap. Ignoring the injuries, Troy hovered over the fallen Miguel Ángel like a Mixed Martial Arts champion, his former friend woozy and bewildered while the crowd chanted "In-fa-mous. ... In-fa-mous ...In-fa-mous."

Troy glanced at Gabriela and Diego. Their vibe was intense: Diego celebrating like the Suns just won the NBA finals; Gabriela with that look of death. The trigger of a gun. *Bang. Bang. Bang.* It passed through his mind and he knew she was thinking the same thing, too. More bloodshed. More violence to come. *Gabby, you better turn away if you don't want to watch what's about to happen next.*

When AC/DC's *Thunderstruck* came on, he flexed his shoulders and embraced the crowd.

The chanting persisted.

Slowly, as though choreographed with the music, he turned to confront Juan Carlos who stood on the viewing platform with Mistah Krunch.

Yo, what's it feel like to be a loser?

The gang leader had his arms crossed and his mouth was twisted in rage.

Staring down the thug, and feeling the music (yeah, his theme song if Juan hadn't figured it out by now) Troy reached behind his head and slowly peeled away the mask to reveal his battered, yet recognizable face.

The music cut off.

The chanting fizzled.

And Juan's eyes popped from their sockets.

"I am the Infamous One," Troy shouted to the crowd. Seemed not a single person had left their seat. "The player formally known as The Outlaw. I am the true undefeated cage champion of the Sonoran Desert. My record stands at 15-0. With six wins by knockout." His eyes returned to Juan. "But I didn't come here to win. I came here—"

Someone shouted, "The Outlaw lives!"

Troy dropped the bloody mask onto the hardwood.

"My brother," he shouted, "... played his heart out on this basketball court, but lost. Two days later, he was murdered." He pulled the Glock from the bellyband and flashed the gun in the air. "For someone here—*for the killer*—it's game over. Because I know who you are. And I've come for justice."

Troy stepped around Miguel's fallen body, the backboard glass and scattered diamonds crunching beneath his shoes, and looked directly into the guy's bruised face.

"Billy trusted you," he said, an impulse from pulling the trigger. "But you betrayed him."

Miguel was in a state of shock. Maybe it was having a loaded gun pointed directly in his face. Maybe it was seeing Troy face to face.

"I swear—"

"You were there," Troy went on. "At my house. The day he died."

"Yes, but—"

"It was you."

"No. You got this wrong, Troy. I didn't do it."

"Who then? If you didn't kill him, who?"

"I can explain."

"Talk then. You got thirty seconds." I unlock the firing

204

mechanism. "It better be the truth."

Miguel struggled to sit. It looked like his wrist was broken. "Your brother came to this basketball court," he said, biting back the pain. "He joined the tournament. He had his sights on being the champ."

"He wanted to beat you."

"Yes."

"For what you did to me last season."

"Yes."

"For how you destroyed my life."

"Yes." Miguel trembled. "I'm sure that was his reason."

Gabriella pushed up against the fence. "Don't do it," she begged.

Unrelenting, Troy said, "Time's up. You talk to slow."

He smacked Miguel with the butt of the handgun, knocking him to the floor, blood spilling from his mouth.

Miguel held up his hands to protect his face from another blow, and said weakly, "You have the wrong guy. It wasn't me."

"Then what were you doing at my house? The day Billy died?"

"I was there," he began, begging for mercy. "But it's not what you think."

"Oh, really?"

"It all started a few months ago." Miguel winced with bloodstained teeth. "Billy saw what was happening at the Mix and wanted in. Like you said, 'brotherly payback' for what we did to you. But also I think he had something to prove."

"Don't we all?"

Dead silence in the arena.

Everyone watching.

Listening.

Miguel wiped blood from the corner of his mouth. "He had developed bigtime ball handling skills," he went on. "Billy could shoot the lights out. That night, he was just too much ... too much for me."

"He *would have* beat you."

"Yes."

"But bogus fouls were called against him. Anything to protect your lead."

"Yeah, that was how it played out."

"So, what happened?"

Miguel looked apologetic. "Billy went home," he explained. "Instead of letting it go, he talked a lot of trash. On the street. On social media—"

"Can you blame him?"

Miguel shook his head. "No. But he pissed off his enemies. The worst kind of enemies." He looked at Juan. The kingpin was standing near the gate. "Powerful men. And to disrespect them?"

Juan threw his hands up in sarcasm, and said, "Hey, don't look at me, amigo. I had no problem with your brother. There may have been some questionable calls. But they went both ways. You know how the game is played."

Miguel moved to his knees. "A lot of money was riding on the final score," he claimed. "How much? Hundreds of thousands? Maybe?"

"Oh, sure, a few bets were placed," Juan admitted, approaching the gate, and stepping onto the court. "However, I assure you, the Elite Mix is a legitimate enterprise."

Looking at Troy, Miguel said, "Several local businessmen bet on Billy. And they got burned. When your brother stoked the fires by claiming the game was fixed, it put too much pressure on The Macho Boys."

Juan shook his head. "More lies. Muchacho won fair and square."

"Juan and his thugs decided to pay Billy a visit," Miguel claimed. "I don't think the plan was to kill him. More like rough him up. You know, payback for all the trash talk."

Juan had restless eyes. He wanted to shut Miguel up, but was helpless. "Take your redemption," he shouted at Troy. "This is what you came here for. Defend your family's honor. Shoot the liar. Shoot the man who killed your brother."

"Shut up," Troy shouted back. "Just shut the hell up."

Too much talking.

Juan.

Miguel.

And the two-headed monster screaming in his head, "pull the trigger," and then "No, put down the gun."

"I went to Douglas," Miguel said. "I searched for him: at the school, at the playground, at the pizza place. Finally, I drove to your house. But I was too late. The house was already on fire. And then I found Billy chained to the basketball pole. He was badly beaten, but alive. I did the best I could to help him. I took his cell phone and dialed 911. And stayed there as long as I could, encouraging him to hold on, until I saw the firetruck coming up the road. I didn't want to get busted, so split. I'm sorry."

Troy moaned.

His former friend had always been a good liar. Why believe him now? Even with a one-percent margin for error, the mountain of evidence was stacked against him.

Rubbing his forehead, a vision of Captain Radanovich appeared before Troy's mind, "Keep the faith," he heard the stern man's lasting words of encouragement. "Everything will turn out good for you. You're a winner." Like a light coming on, the absurdity of the present situation flashed before his eyes, the danger of having slipped back to his former ways, allowing the rage, the volatile anger, the payback mindset to get the best of him. Once again, his inner struggles threatened to tear down his dreams. *People are counting on you to do the right thing.* Not only his mother, but his friends, and importantly he owed himself some respect.

Yet, here you are, victorious and pointing a gun at Miguel. Have you learned nothing?

He suddenly saw the senselessness of everything. Rogue justice won't bring Billy back. "Walk away," he whispered. "You can do better."

His shooting hand shaking, he lowered to a knee and placed the gun on the floor and pushed it away.

Truth?

Or lies.

It didn't matter.

"I'm sorry," Miguel whispered. "The last couple of years I was only jealous of your basketball success."

Juan walked over and placed a foot on the gun. With an arrogant grin, he clapped hands and nodded passionately. "Well, well, well ..." Then to the stunned audience, he asked, "Better than Shakespeare, no?"

But the crowd was growing uneasy.

"The ruby is missing," P-Brain interrupted frantically. He had been scrambling across the floor and searching for the rich gemstone. "I can't find it."

"You stupid fool," Juan snapped. "It can't be missing."

"But it is."

"Keep looking."

"I've searched."

"Search again."

Now Krunch pointed at Troy, and said, "Yo, I saw Blake pick something up. Check him out."

Juan leaned over and grabbed the Glock. "Troy Blake?" he asked directly, pointing the weapon. "Where is my ruby?"

"I don't have it."

"Don't even mess with me, gringo."

"I said—"

Suddenly the sound of whistles pierced the air. Several police officers stormed into the warehouse from the main entrance. A bust, Troy thought quickly, hearing people scream and watching the crowd disperse. He sure as heck didn't want to stick around to see what happened next.

Juan looked over his shoulder, then to Krunch, and said, "Fuck."

At that moment, Troy kicked Juan in the nuts and sent him to a knee. After flashing the red ruby in his hand he made a fist and wacked the guy across the chin, then started for the gate where Diego was shouting, "C'mon, dude, let's roll!"

Troy darted through the panicked crowd. "Follow me," he said to Diego and Gabriela. "I know another way."

The arena's overhead lights had come on and cops were using bullhorns to order people to vacate the building. Looking over his shoulder, he saw Mistah Krunch locked in handcuffs. And P-Brain trapped inside the cage.

Charging up the red-carpet, he entered the behind-the-scenes corridor and passed by the makeshift locker room, and then sprinted toward the rear exit. Surprisingly, they were alone. Seemed everyone in the building—except for maybe the three of them—was obeying the demands of the police.

Troy reached for the door handle. Just go out the back way, he thought. *Run across the basketball court. Climb the fence. Then disappear into the night.* Instead of turning the handle, and rushing outside, he paused to listen. It sounded like cops yelling; a man's voice shouting in Spanish, and pounding on the door, "Police, open up."

Crap, Troy thought. Now what?

He couldn't return to the arena. The cops were busting things up. Dressed in a basketball uniform and with blood on his face, he stood apart from the spectators. *How many cell phones had captured him pointing a gun at Miguel?*

Nearby, Gabriela stood at another door with a sign that read ESCALERA, and shouted, "The stairs. C'mon. Let's take 'em."

Troy entered the stairwell and climbed to the third floor. Maybe they could find a closet and hide? *Wait things out.* Exiting the stairwell, he suddenly found himself standing across the hall from Juan Carlos.

The kingpin was attempting to evade the cops, too. He flashed the Glock handgun. "I want my ruby," Juan shouted. "Give it to me!"

"Take it easy," Troy said. "We can work this out."

They stepped away from Juan, slowly backing up.

"The ruby," Juan demanded. "Hand it over. And I won't harm you."

"Can't. It's hidden somewhere in the arena," Troy insisted, noticing someone had cracked open the stairwell's door. "In a trashcan by the cage."

"What?"

"I didn't want the cops to have it."

"Which trash can?"

"Put the gun down, dude. I'll tell you."

"No." He fired a shot in the air. "Tell me now."

"Hold on. Wait a sec."

"Listen to me, gringo. Don't make me do to you what I did to your brother."

"What *you* did?"

"You heard me."

"So ... you killed Billy?"

"Are you stupid?" Juan shook his head. "Of course, I killed Billy. With my own bare hands. And I enjoyed every punch."

"You son-of-a—"

Another fired shot, the bullet zipping above Troy's head and stopping his charge. "Miguel told the truth," Juan confessed. "Now he's nothing more than trash. Completely disposable. I used him, like I use all the other players in my league—to make money." He flashed a taunting grin. "His next game, after my boys get done with him, will be in a dumpster."

Juan pointed the gun at Troy. Before he could pull the trigger, Miguel emerged from the stairwell and tackled him to the floor. It only took three punches and the kingpin was out cold.

Miguel held up a cell phone. "A dumpster, huh?" he said, his eye black and puffy. "Actually, it's game over for you—Juan Carlos. I just recorded your confession."

"I—" Troy started to apologize, realizing he had almost killed his innocent friend on the basketball court.

But Miguel blurted, "You better get out of here. Cops are on their way."

"Come with us," Troy said, picking up the handgun.

"No. I'm tired of running. Besides, I need to get this video to the police." Miguel pointed to an open door located at the end of the hall. "There's a fire escape in that office."

Hearing the cops charging up the stairwell, Miguel scrambled through the door to surrender, buying Troy and his friends time to flee.

Entering a large room filled with expensive furniture, and an open wall safe, they scooted past a desk and bolted for a window.

Gabriela pushed it up.

Then, one after the other each climbed onto a metal platform and reached for a rickety ladder attached to the brick wall. Climbing down, Troy was last to drop to the pavement.

Standing on the dark street, it seemed the coast was clear until speeding headlights approached.

"Crap," Troy said. "More cops." If caught with a firearm, he would spend more than a night in jail. So he ditched the handgun into a nearby dumpster.

"Wait a second," Gabriella shot back with a hand in the air. "It's my uncle."

Suddenly the Metal Church Bus roared to a stop in front of their feet and the door swung open. "Going my way?" Peavey asked sarcastically, the sound of Queensrÿche jamming from the stereo.

"What the—?" Troy said. "Peavey is your uncle?"

"Yeah. Why, do you know him?"

"Uh, sort of." Rushing in, he high-fived the roadie, and said, "Take us home, bro."

Peavey grinned and closed the door with the lever by the steering wheel. "You won, brother. Just as I had hoped. And I'm not talking about the final score."

His heart racing, Troy sat in a seat near his friends, leaning back against the cushion with a heavy breath. Thanks to Miguel's video, Billy won, too. *Mission complete.* He looked at his basketball shoes: the ruby made a small lump in a sock, where—*for now*—it was safe and secure.

Making **Peace**

In the days that followed, Miguel concocted the perfect story about how he and Troy had planned the one-on-one game to get a confession. From jail in Agua Prieta, he claimed the gun was a stage prop—a lie clearly meant to save Troy's butt.

"We weren't sure if Juan would fall for the trap," Troy told Sgt. Jones. "Guess it worked out okay." He hadn't spoken to his ex-friend since punishing him on the hardwood, so was careful to avoid details that might contradict the story.

"And the gun?" Jones looked him dead on. "A prop like Miguel claims?"

"Yup." Troy leaned back in a chair. More lies, but it helped the Glock had disappeared. The truth, that he had pointed a loaded weapon at Miguel and threatened to shoot, could launch attempted murder charges plus a host of other crimes on both sides of the border. Exhaling, he added, "We were just acting."

"From the videos I've seen ... all that blood ... the fighting ... I'd say you were doing more than just acting."

"Well, the basketball game was legit."

"A bit rough though, eh?"

"It's the only way we play."

"Mmm ..." The police officer glanced at paperwork on the desk. "Had it been a real gun, you'd be in serious trouble."

Troy gulped. "Good thing it wasn't."

"Taking the law into y   was foolish."

"I know. Promise you.

"Let's hope so."

Troy nodded, and asked, "What about Miguel? Will they prosecute him?"

"Playing basketball isn't a crime. Neither is fighting on a basketball court." Jones raised an eyebrow. "Stupid, but not criminal." He winked, easing the tension. "I've spoken to my counterparts in Agua Prieta. Miguel is cooperating with investigators. That's a good start. Plus, he helped bring down one of Sonora's most notorious drug dealers."

"Wish somehow ... I could help."

"In the end, things should work out for him. Plus, his grandfather is a retired politician from Hermosillo. He'll have something to say about this."

"That's good then."

It felt more like a farewell than an interrogation. Jones reached for his coffee cup, and said, "Well, Mr. Blake, as of right now, we have no more business to discuss. There's no need to let this incident in Mexico prevent you from pursuing your dreams."

"Thank you, sir."

"I assume you've met with the Cochise County Probation Office?"

"I have."

"Excellent. Then it looks like you're free to go."

"Sweet," Troy said, shaking hands before jetting out the door.

Surprisingly, except for short mention that Mexican police had a suspect in the murder of Billy Blake, the bust in Agua Prieta never made headlines in the Douglas newspapers. With Juan behind bars there was a sense that everyone had just sort of moved on—waiting for the big trial that was sure to come.

In May, humbled and drug-free, authorities released Miguel from a Mexican jail and he returned to Douglas to work at his father's car lot.

A couple days later, Troy, who had been staying with Diego and Gabriela, went to apologize for mistaking him for his brother's killer. And to thank him for working up the genius lie about the gun.

"I think they've pretty much bought into the prop story," Miguel said. "And because I've agreed to testify against Juan, everything seems pretty cool for now."

Troy knew the decision to oppose Juan in a court of law would put a mark on Miguel's back. "Things could get ugly."

"It's the right thing to do. Especially for Billy."

Troy patted his friend on the shoulder—a gesture of appreciation.

They spoke for a while longer, about Billy, how Miguel felt guilty for not staying with him until the ambulance arrived. With customers entering the car lot, they quickly re-lived their epic game at the Mix.

"But seriously, dude, you got away with a travel on that last play," Miguel said.

"What? Heck no."

"Next time you won't be so lucky."

"Yo. Anytime. Name the day."

Miguel smirked. "Good luck, bro."

"You, too."

They slapped hands and then Troy climbed into the truck and cranked the ignition. He had already said goodbye to his mother, his friends, and Coach Chavez.

Setting his phone into a plastic holder on the dashboard, he opened the Google maps app and headed north on the highway.

The **Walk** On

I remember something Jimmy had said a few days after his suicide attempt, when he was thankful to be alive. "Life," he'd said to me, "always offers you a second chance. It starts with tomorrow."

The solid advice was taken to heart; I realize second chances don't mean squat if you don't learn from your first mistakes.

And so now *my tomorrow* has come.

Four months after that battle with Miguel, I arrive at a mid-major basketball program in eastern Washington, a good school willing to give a fallen hoopster like me a second chance. My pencil sharpened, I'm focused and prepared for summer session and for any unseen challenges that fly my way. But first, I need to pass a couple of prerequisite classes before I am officially admitted to the university.

I study hard and ace my exams.

Then, in September, when fall term begins and the basketball team shows up, I join their practices and work my butt off. First to show, last to leave, shooting four hundred free throws a day. I've never worked harder for anything in my life.

The competition at point guard is intense. Me versus the team's returning starter, plus throw into the mix a senior All-Conference shooting guard who's looking to impress NBA scouts by picking up some minutes at the helm.

I'm not backing down.

Never have.

This morning, the very day we board a plane and fly to North Carolina to play Duke at Cameron Indoor Stadium coach calls me to his office. "Congratulations," he says.

"For what?"

"You've earned the starting job."

"Seriously?"

He gives me a fist bump. "And we're working on a scholarship for you."

I'm pretty jacked up.

Leaving his office, I don't remember what I said in response (did I even thank him?) but I'm already texting Chavez, Gabriela, Diego, Jackson, Jimmy, and my mom the big news.

Clean-shaven and wearing shorts and a t-shirt, with a backpack over my shoulder, I drop sunglasses on my nose and high-five a guy who lives in my dorm.

"Good luck this weekend," he says.

I have to quick stop by the campus bookstore to purchase Dante's *Inferno* for Italian Humanities class.

On the way, I grab my iPhone and surf to espn.com. A college hoops analyst has already tweeted out the lineup change, something about me being a former Top 100 player turned walk-on. Yet, even with our "underrated backcourt" getting some love, the pre-game breakdown gives us zero chance of beating Duke. The Blue Devils are the number one ranked team in the country. Three of their starters are projected to go in the first round of the NBA draft. This Saturday, on national television, with my family and friends watching from their living rooms, we are huge underdogs. But, hey, what do the *experts* know? I like our chances. My goal isn't to lead the team to a respectable showing; it's to win.

Even though the hard work has paid off, playing D1 ball and working toward a scholarship isn't the real reason why I came here.

It's strange to admit, but for the first time in my life I can honestly say that some things matter more than basketball. Well, one thing, anyway.

Emma.

I can't stop thinking about her.

Fall classes have been going for seven weeks and I've yet to run into her. Strange, because it's not that big a campus. The laws of probability suggest we should have bumped into each other by now.

Then again, it shouldn't come as a surprise because my student athlete routine keeps me from socializing. In fact, I spend most of my time at the gym, studying in the library, watching film, and working on my jump shot.

I'm fearful, too. In the back of my mind, I've been thinking: as long as I don't run into Emma, I won't find out if she's really back with Peter. I know, I know. What a coward, right?

Halfway to the bookstore, I get a text from Jimmy.

BEAT DUKE!

Attached to the text is a photo of Jimmy sitting on his new motorcycle—*his dream ride*. I know all about the bike because shortly before leaving Douglas, I returned to Mexico one last time. My new friend Ignacio knows a shady dude named Arturo who happens to deal in gems and precious metals. Arturo has an undisclosed office somewhere in town. Me and Ignacio were blindfolded and taken to him.

The encounter was scary, Arturo sitting in shadows, surrounded by armed thugs, everyone looking at me like I wasn't going to leave the place alive.

Surprisingly, a few minutes into what I figured was "certain death" turned into a high-five conversation about heavy metal and classic rock. As it turns out, Arturo is a huge fan of rock music memorabilia, a collector of priceless guitars, famous band costumes, and autographs. He is friends with some of history's most notable singers, guitarists, and drummers. After we shared the list of concerts we'd attended (of course, he's seen pretty much everyone, and in stadiums all over the world), he wanted to know how much I was asking for the prize ruby and I replied just the price of a "special motorcycle for a friend." With one condition: that it was shipped to Alaska anonymously, along with a letter stating Jimmy had won it in a competition.

Other than that, I didn't take a dime. The ruby wasn't mine to keep, but like a modern-day Robin Hood I wanted something for my Cajun pal. Is that so wrong?

I send back a thumbs-up emoji with a big grin on my face as I picture him on one of his cross-country rides.

Now I'm thinking about the big game versus Duke when, arriving to the bookstore, I suddenly glance up from the phone and feel my heart skip. It's Emma. She is exiting the door.

Uh-oh.

Didn't expect this.

What should I do?

Run?

I stop dead in my tracks when like a door slamming on my face I notice this guy she's standing with. When she gives him a hug, it confirms my worst fears: there is nothing—probably never was anything—between us.

Just as I start to back away, she looks at me like she knows who I am. But how could she? I'm wearing sunglasses and don't have a beard.

"Troy?" she says.

"Uh, Emma?"

"Oh my gosh, what are you doing here?"

"Going to the bookstore," I mumble stupidly, feeling more like her stalker than a friend.

"You're a student? Here?"

"Uh-huh."

She walks toward me, pulling the other guy along by the hand, until she lets go and rushes into my open arms. I wasn't expecting this. *Cool!* I wrap her up like there's no tomorrow. By far, it's the best squeeze I've ever felt. Heck—ever given.

"I've missed you," she says. That smile already working its magic. "What happened?"

"Didn't you get my note?"

"What note?"

"I left it at the café."

"No. I didn't get it." She steps back. "When you didn't show up, I quit. I was pretty bummed out."

"Sorry. Something happened. I tried to find you but Alice said you were back with—"

"Damn Alice. She thinks she's my mother."

"So Peter?"

"We broke up."

I'm confused. Then who's the dude? She must have noticed my eyes and read my exact thoughts. "This is my brother Thomas," she finally says. "It's his birthday."

"Your brother?"

"Hey," Thomas says, but adds he has to go or he'll be late for class.

After he walks away, Emma says, "Funny, a friend of mine said there was some new basketball player on the team named Troy who is really, really good." Her eyes grow big. "Is that—?"

"Yup. In the flesh."

221

Taking the **Stage**

Game day. Saturday night, and I'm in the locker room fighting off the pre-game jitters. This always happens. When I was a kid, I used to hyperventilate before games. Now I've learned to accept and manage my anxiety. It's part of who I am. Filter the pressure. In with it. Out with it. *You take on the world when you step onto the court*. Once the game tips off the anxiety will disappear and my focus and athleticism will be in check.

In the meantime, to calm these passing fears, I'm pumping up my teammates by saying positive things and making sure each player believes in himself. "Underdogs exist only on paper," I remind them. "We came here to win."

"Hit the floor," coach shouts.

Heck yeah. My moment has finally arrived. I've been dreaming about playing big time ball since grade school.

Walking into Duke's storied arena is like an out of body experience. The sea of blue. The championship banners. The media circus. How cool is this environment? Not every player gets to kick-start his college career on national television versus the best team in the country. High-fiving my teammates before tip-off, I'm thinking I wouldn't have it any other way.

From the moment we lose the jump ball, Duke is all over us. The Blue Demons play unselfishly and hit their open shots like a well-oiled machine.

Quickly up 10 – 0, the Cameron Crazies cheering in the stands come down hard on us, shattering the Richter scale, holding up signs (one of them shows my face behind jail bars), and waving white sticks in an effort to break our concentration at the free throw line. Seriously, how close are they to the court? It doesn't seem legit by the rules.

We're rattled and fall behind by 16 early on.

Coach uses a timeout to draw up a play, urging us to keep fighting, to "pass the ball" and to "find an open man." Thanks to our bench we methodically narrow the gap to 8 points by halftime.

... we're in this.

In the locker room, coach lays into us for not rebounding and for not playing up-tempo ball. We have a platoon of pure shooters on this team. J.R. from Coos Bay. Sayer from Puyallup. Marks from Tacoma. Three-star athletes, but five-star guys at heart. I know we can run and gun with the best of 'em—even Duke.

"Doubt," I tell Marks, "is the greatest enemy."

Frustrated over his poor shooting, Marks raises his chin.

After slapping hands, the guys start for the hardwood. Coach is looking at me. I know what he's thinking: *this is your team, take control.*

The Duke players are cold to start the second half. They miss a few easy shots and turn the ball over multiple times. Now my teammates are starting to believe in the possibility of leaving Cameron with a win.

Back and forth.
Back and forth.
It's a battle.

When we take our first lead with three minutes to play in the game, I push the tempo up another notch, drawing a fifth foul on their All-American guard, and then make sure we break their press.

Our team's composure down the stretch is insane. All that noise. The taunting from the fans. I'm at the free throw line when some rowdy shouts out, "jailbird," as I sink the second of two.

By now, coach has removed his jacket and his shirt's armpits are drenched in sweat.

Believe.

Don't let up.

Finish this off!

At the buzzer, after our hard fought 88-84 upset victory, I chuck the basketball into the air and celebrate with my teammates.

Coach's celebration lasts for about ten seconds. He's already moved on and invites me to stand with him to field questions from the television media.

"You might be a household name by tomorrow morning," a woman ESPN reporter says to me, mentioning my 15 points, 12 assists, 6 steals, and only 1 turnover stats. "But I remember you. A few years ago, you were one of the top prospects in the country. Where have you been all this time?"

"Fishing," I reply.

The reporter and cameraman smile.

"No seriously," she says, "where have you been?"

"In Alaska. Fishing." I can't help but look at the camera and give a shout out to Emma on the other side.

"Well, you shredded the Blue Devil defense with your quickness and sharp passes," she says. "And you played with four fouls for most of the second half."

"I can reel it back when necessary."

"You sure can." She smiles, and before sticking the microphone back in my face, asks, "So how does it feel to knock off the number one team in the country?"

I'm not sure what to say.

It all seems so unreal.

Me standing here.

In the lights.

On live television.

True, it's one of the biggest college basketball upsets in recent years. But I sense, it's only the beginning of a magical season that's destined to reach the Final Four.

www.ingramcontent.com/pod-product-compliance
Lightning Source LLC
Chambersburg PA
CBHW021031130626
46552CB00005B/1779